William Shakespeare, Charles Praetorius, Peter A. Daniel

The Life and Death of King Richard the Second

William Shakespeare, Charles Praetorius, Peter A. Daniel

The Life and Death of King Richard the Second

ISBN/EAN: 9783337388232

Printed in Europe, USA, Canada, Australia, Japan

Cover: Foto ©Andreas Hilbeck / pixelio.de

More available books at **www.hansebooks.com**

THE
LIFE AND DEATH OF KING
RICHARD THE SECOND.

BY

WILLIAM SHAKESPEARE.

Qo. 5, 1634.

A FACSIMILE IN PHOTO-LITHOGRAPHY
BY
CHARLES PRAETORIUS,

WITH AN INTRODUCTORY NOTICE
BY
P. A. DANIEL.

———◆———

LONDON:
PRODUCED BY C. PRAETORIUS, 14 CLAREVILLE GROVE,
HEREFORD SQUARE, S.W.
1887.

43 SHAKSPERE QUARTO FACSIMILES,

WITH INTRODUCTIONS, LINE-NUMBERS, &C., BY SHAKSPERE SCHOLARS,

ISSUED UNDER THE SUPERINTENDENCE OF DR. F. J. FURNIVALL.

1. *Those by W. Griggs.*

No.
1. Hamlet. 1603. Q1.
2. Hamlet. 1604. Q2.
3. Midsummer Night's Dream. 1600. (Fisher.)
4. Midsummer Night's Dream. 1600. (Roberts.)
5. Loves Labor's Lost. 1598. Q1.
6. Merry Wives. 1602. Q1.
7. Merchant of Venice. 1600. Q1. (Roberts.)
8. Henry IV, 1st Part. 1598. Q1.

No.
9. Henry IV. 2nd Part. 1600. Q1.
10. Passionate Pilgrim. 1599. Q1.
11. Richard III. 1597. Q1.
12. Venus and Adonis. 1593. Q1.
13. Troilus and Cressida. 1609. Q1.
17. Richard II. 1597. Q1. Duke of Devonshire's copy. (*on stone.*)

2. *Those by C. Praetorius.*

14. Much Ado About Nothing. 1600. Q1.
15. Taming of a Shrew. 1594. Q1.
16. Merchant of Venice. 1600. Q2. (Heyes.)
18. Richard II. 1597. Q1. Mr. Huth's copy. (*on stone.*)
19. Richard II. 1608. Q3. (*on stone.*)
20. Richard II. 1634. Q5.
21. Pericles. 1609. Q1.
22. Pericles. 1609. Q2.
23. The Whole Contention. 1619. Q3. Part I. (for 2 Henry VI.).
24. The Whole Contention. 1619. Q3. Part II. (for 3 Henry VI.).
25. Romeo and Juliet. 1597. Q1.
26. Romeo and Juliet. 1599. Q2.
27. Henry V. 1600. Q1.
28. Henry V. 1608. Q2.
29. Titus Andronicus. 1600. Q1.

30. Sonnets and Lover's Complaint. 1609. Q1.
31. Othello. 1622. Q1.
32. Othello. 1630. Q2.
33. King Lear. 1608. Q1. (N. Butter, *Pide Bull.*)
34. King Lear. 1608. Q2. (N. Butter.)
35. Rape of Lucrece. 1594. Q1.
36. Romeo and Juliet. Undated.
37. Contention. 1594. (For 2 Henry VI.)
38. True Tragedy. 1595. (For 3 Henry VI.)
39. The Famous Victories of Henry V. 1598.
40. The Troublesome Raigne of King John. Part I. 1591.
41. The Troublesome Raigne of King John. Part II. 1591. Q1.
42. Richard III. 1602. C3. (*In progress.*)
43. Richard III. 1622. Q6. (*fotograft.*)

THE
LIFE AND
DEATH OF KING
RICHARD THE
SECOND.

With new Additions of the
Parliament Scene, and the
Depoſing of King *Richard*.

As it hath beene acted by the Kings Majeſties
Servants, at the *Globe*.

By *William Shakeſpeare*.

LONDON,
Printed by IOHN NORTON.
1634.

The Life and Death of
King *Richard* the fecond.

Actus Primus, Scæna Prima.

Enter King Richard, Iohn a Gaunt, with other
Nobles, and Attendants.

King Richard

Ld *Iohn* of *Gaunt*, time-honoured *Lancaster*,
Haft thou according to thy oath and band,
Brought hither *Henry Hereford*, thy bold fon:
Here to make good, the boyfterous late appeale
Which then our leafure would not let vs heare,
Againft the Duke of *Norfolke, Thomas Mowbray*?

Gaunt. I haue my Liege.

King. Tell me moreouer, haft thou founded him,
If he appeale the Duke on ancient malice,
Or worthily as a good fubiect fhould,
On fome knowne ground of treachery in him.

Gaunt. As neere as I could fift him on that argument,
On fome apparant danger feene in him,
Aym'd at your highneffe, no inueterate malice.

King. Then call them to our prefence face to face,
And frowning brow to brow, our felues will heare
Th' accufer, and the accufed, freely fpeake;
High ftomack'd are they both, and full of ire
In rage, deafe as the fea; hafty as fire.

A 2   *Enter*

4

Enter Bullingbrooke, and Mowbray.

20   *Bul.* Many yeeres of happy dayes befall
My gracious Soveraigne, my loving Liege.
    Mow. Each day ſtill better others happineſſe,
Vntill the heavens enuying earths good hap,
24   Adde an immortall title to your Crowne.
    King. We thanke you both, yet one but flatters vs,
As well appeareth by the cauſe you come,
Namely to appeale each other of high treaſon.
28   Coſin of *Hereford*, what doſt thou obiect
Againſt the Duke of *Norfolke*, *Thomas Mowbray* ?
    Bul. Firſt, (heaven be the record of my ſpeech,)
In the devotion of a ſubiects love,
32   Tendring the precious ſafety of my Prince,
And free from other miſ-begotten hate,
†   Come I appelant to his Princely preſence.
Now *Thomas Mowbray*, doe I turne to thee,
36   And marke my greeting well: for what I ſpeake,
My body ſhall make good upon this earth,
Or my divine Soule anſwer it in Heaven.
Thou art a Traytor, and a miſcreant ;
40   Too good to be ſo, and too bad to live,
Since the more faire and Chriſtall is the Skie,
The uglier ſeemes the Clouds, that in it flye :
Once more, the more to aggravate the note,
44   With a foule traitors name, ſtuffe I thy throat,
And wiſh (ſo pleaſe my Soveraigne) ere I move,
What my tongue ſpeakes, my right drawne ſword may prove.
    Mow. Let not my coole words here accuſe my zeale
48   'Tis not the tryall of a womans warre,
The bitter clamour of two eager tongues,
Can arbitrate this cauſe betwixt us twaine :
The blood is hot that muſt be cool'd for this,
52   Yet can I not of ſuch tame patience boaſt,
As to be huſht, and nought at all to ſay.
Firſt, the faire reverence of your Highneſſe curbes me,
From giving reines and ſpurres to my free ſpeech,
† 56   Which once would poſt, untill it had return'd

                       Theſe

Theſe termes of treaſon, doubly downe his throat.
Setting aſide his high bloods royalty,
And let him be no kinſman to my Liege,
I doe defie him, and I ſpit at him,
Call him a ſlandrous Coward, and a Villaine:
Which to maintaine, I would allow him oddes,
And meet him, were I tide to runne a foote,
Even to the frozen ridges of the Alpes,
Or any other ground inhabitable,
Where ever Engliſh man durſt ſet his foote.
Meane time, let this defend my royalty,
By all my hopes moſt falſely doth he lye.

   Bul. Pale trembling Coward, there I throw my gage,
Diſclaiming here the kindred of the King,
And lay aſide my high bloods royalty,
Which feare, not reverence makes me to except,
If guilty dread have left thee ſo much ſtrength,
As to take up mine honours pawne, then ſtoope,
By that, and all the rights of Knighthood elſe,
Will I make good againſt thee arme to arme,
What I have ſpoken, or thou canſt deviſe.

   Mow. I take it up, and by that ſword I ſweare,
Which gently layd my Knighthood on my ſhoulder,
Ile anſwer thee in any faire degree,
Or Chivalrous deſigne of Knightly tryall :
And when I mount, alive may I not light,
If I be traytor, or unjuſtly fight.

   King. What doth our Coſin lay to *Mowbrayes* charge ?
It muſt be great that can inherite us,
So much as of a thought of ill in him.

   Bul. Looke what I ſayd my life ſhall prove it true,
That *Mowbray* hath receiv'd eight thouſand Nobles,
In name of lendings for your highneſſe Souldiers,
The which he hath detain'd for lewd imployments,
Like a falſe Traytor, and iniurious Villaine.
Beſides I ſay, and will in battell prove,
Or here or elſewhere to the furtheſt Verge
That ever was ſurvey'd by Engliſh eye,

      That

The Life and Death

That all the treasons of these eighteene yeares
Complotted and contrived in this Land,
Fetcht from false *Mowbray* their first head and spring.
Further I say and further will maintaine
Vpon his bad life, to make all this good,
That he did plot the Duke of *Glosters* death,
Suggest his soone beleeving adversaries,
And consequently like a Traytor Coward,
Sluc'd out his innocent soule through streames of blood:
Which blood, like sacrificing *Abels* cryes,
(Even from the tonguelesse cavernes of the earth)
To me for Iustice, and rough chasticement:
And by the glorious worth of my descent,
This arme shall doe it, or this life be spent

   King. How high a pitch his resolution soares;
Thomas of *Norfolke*, what sayest thou to this ?
   Mow. Oh let my soveraigne turne away his face,
And bid his eares a little while be deafe,
Till I have told this slander of his blood,
How God and good men hate so fowle a lyer.
   King. Mowbray, impartiall are our eyes and eares,
Were he our brother, nay, our Kingdomes heire,
As he is but our fathers brothers sonne ;
Now by my Scepters awe, I make a vow,
Such neighbour-neerenesse to our sacred blood,
Should nothing priviledge him, nor partialize
The unstooping firmenesse of our upright soule.
He is our subiect (*Mowbray*) so art thou,
Free speech and fearelesse, I to thee allow.
   Mow. Then *Bullingbrooke* as low as to thy heart,
Through the false passage of thy throat; thou lyest:
Three parts of that receipt I had for Callice,
Disburst I to his Highnesse souldiers :
The other part reserv'd I by consent,
For that my soveraigne Liege was in my debt,
Vpon remainder of a deare account,
Since last I went to *France* to fetch his Queene:
Now swallow downe that lye. For *Glosters* death,

I

of Richard *the second.*

I flew him not ; but (to mine owne difgrace)
Neglected my fworne duty in that cafe :
For you my Noble Lord of Lancafter,
The honourable father to my foe,
Once I did lay an ambufh for your life,
A trefpaffe that doth vex my grieved foule:
But ere I laft receiv'd the Sacrament,
I did confeffe it, and exactly begg'd
Your Graces pardon, and I hope I had it.
This is my fault: as for the reft appeal'd,
It iffues from the rancour of a villaine,
A recreant, and moft degenerate Traytor.
Which in my felfe I boldly will defend,
And enterchangeably hurle downe my gage,
Vpon this overweening Traitors foot,
To prove my felfe a loyall Gentleman,
Even in the beft blood chamber'd in his bofome.
In hafte whereof moft heartily I pray
Your Highneffe to affigne our tryall day.

  King. Wrath kindled Genlemen be rul'd by me:
Let's purge this choller without letting blood :
This we prefcribe , though no Phyfition.
Deepe malice makes too deepe incifion.
Forget, forgive, conclude, and be agreed,
Our Doctors fay, this is no time to bleed.
Good Vncle, let this end where it begun,
Wee'l calme the Duke of *Norfolke*, you your fonne.

  Gaunt. To be a make-peace fhall become my age,
Throw downe (my fonne) the Duke of *Norfolkes* gage.

  King. And *Norfolke*, throw downe his.

  Gaunt. When *Harry* when? Obedience bids,
Obedience bids, I fhould not bid agen.

  King. Norfolke, throw downe, we bid; there is no boote.

  Mow. My felfe I throw (dread Soveraigne) at thy foot.
My life thou fhalt command, but not my fhame,
The one my duty owes, but my faire name
Defpight of death that lives upon my grave
To darke difhonours ufe, thou fhalt not have.

                                      I am

The Life and Death

I am difgrac'd, impeach'd, and baffel'd here,
Pierc'd to the foule with flanders venom'd fpeare:
The which no Balme can cure, but his heart blood
Which breath'd this poyfon.

King. Rage muft be withftood:
Give me his gage: Lyons make Leopards tame.

Mow. Yea, but not change his fpots: take but my fhame,
And I refigne my gage. My deare, deare Lord,
The pureft treafure mortall times afford,
Is fpotleffe reputation : that away,
Men are but gilded loame, or painted clay.
A jewell in a ten-times barr'd up Cheft,
Is a bold fpirit in a loyall breft.
Mine honour is my life ; both grow in one :
Take honour from me, and my life is done.
Then (deare my Liege) mine honour let me try,
In that I live, and for that will I dye.

King. Cofin throw downe your gage,
Doe you begin.

Bul. Oh heaven defend my foule from fuch foule finne,
Shall I feeme Creft-falne in my fathers fight,
Or with pale beggar-feare impeach my height
Before this out-dar'd daftard? Ere my tongue,
Shall wound mine honour with fuch feeble wrong ;
Or found fo bafe a parle : my teeth fhall teare
The flavifh motive of recanting feare,
And fpit it bleeding in this high difgrace,
Where fhame doth harbour, even in *Mowbrayes* face.

Exit Gaunt.

King. We were not borne to fue, but to command,
Which fince we cannot doe to make you friends,
Be ready, (as your lives fhall anfwer it)
At *Coventree,* upon Saint *Lamberts* day :
There fhall your Swords and Lances arbitrate
The fwelling difference of your fetled hate:
Since we cannot attone you, you fhall fee
Iuftice defigne the Victors Chivalry.
Lord Marfhall, command our Officers at Armes,

Be

Be ready to direct thefe home, Alarmes.   *Exeunt:*

Scæna Secunda.

Enter Gaunt, and Dutcheffe of Glocefter.
Gaunt. Alas, the part I had in *Glofters* blood,
Doth more folicite me than your exclaimes,
To ftirre againft the butchers of his life.
But fince correction lyeth in thofe hands
Which made the fault that we cannot correct,
Put we our quarrell to the will of Heauen,
Who when they fee the houres ripe on earth,
Will raigne hot vengeance on offenders heads.
    Dut. Finds brotherhood in thee no fharper fpurre?
Hath love in thy old blood no liuing fire?
Edwards feven fonnes (whereof thy felfe art one)
Where are feven vialles of his facred blood.
Or feuen faire branches fpringing from one roote:
Some of thofe feuen are dryed by natures courfe,
Some of thofe branches by the deftinies cut:
But *Thomas*, my deare Lord, my life, my *Glofter*,
One Viall full of *Edwards* facred blood,
One flourifhing branch of his moft Royall roote
Is crack'd, and all the precious liquor fpilt;
Is hackt downe, and his fummer leaues all vaded
By Envies hand, and Murders bloody Axe.
Ah *Gaunt*? His blood was thine, that bed, that wombe,
That mettall, that felfe-mould that fafhion'd thee,
Made him a man: and though thou liu'ft and breath'ft;
Yet art thou flaine in him: thou doeft confent
In fome large meafure to thy Fathers death,
In that thou feeft thy wretched brother dy,
Who was the modell of thy Fathers life,
Call it not patience (*Gaunt*) it is defpaire,
In fuffering thus thy brother to be flaughter'd

              B   Thou

The Life and Death

Thou shew'ft the naked pathway to thy life,
Teaching fterne murther how to butcher thee:
That which in meane men we intitle patience
Is pale cold cowardife in noble breafts :
What fhall I fay, to fafegard thine owne life,
The beft way is to venge my *Gloffers* death.
  Gaunt. Heavens is the quarrell : for Heavens fubftitute
His Deputy annoynted in his fight,
Hath caus'd his death, the which if wrongfully
Let heaven revenge : for I may neuer lift
An angry arme againft his Minifter.
  Dut. Where then (alas) may I complaine my felfe?
  Gan.To heaven the widdowes Champion to defence.
  Dut.Why then I will : farewell old *Gaunt*.
Thou go'ft to Coventry, there to behold
Our Cofin *Hereford* , and fell *Mowbray* fight:
O fit my husbands wrongs on *Herefords* fpeare,
That it may enter butcher Mowbrayes breaft :
Or if misfortune miffe the firft carreere,
Be *Mowbrayes* finnes fo heavy in his bofome,
That they may breake his foaming courfers backe,
And throw the Rider headlong in the Lifts,
A Caytiffe recreant to my Cofin *Hereford*.
Farewell old *Gaunt*, thy fometimes brothers wife
With her companion Greefe, muft end her life.
  Gau. Sifter fare well ; I muft to Couentry,
As much good ftay with thee, as go with me.
  Dut. Yet one word more Greefe, boundeth where it
Not with the empty hollowneffe, but weight.   (falls,
I take my leaue before I haue begun,
For forrow ends not : when it feemeth done.
Commend me to my brother *Edward Yorke*.
Loe, this is all : nay yet depart, not fo,
Though this be all , do not fo quickely goe,
I fhall remember more. Bid him, Oh, what ?
With all good fpeed at *Pleſhie* vifite me.
Alacke, and what fhall good old *Yorke* there fee
But empty lodgings, and unfurnifh'd walles,

Vn-

of Richard *the second.*

Vn-peopl'd Offices, untroden ſtones?
And what heare there for welcome, but my groanes?
Therefore commend me, let him not come there,
To ſeeke out ſorrow, that dwels every where:
Deſolate, deſolate will I hence and dye,
The laſt leave of thee, takes my weeping eye.　*Exeunt.*

Scæna Tertia.

Enter Marſhall, and Aumerle.

Mar. My L. *Aumerle,* is *Harry Hereford* arm'd?
Aum. Yea, at all poynts, and longs to enter in.
Mar. The Duke of Norfolke, ſprightfully and bold,
Stayes but the ſummons of the Appellants Trumpet.
Au. Why then the Champions, are prepar'd, and ſtay
For nothing but his Maieſties approach.

　　　　　　　　　　　　　Flouriſh.

Enter King, Gaunt, Buſhy, Bagot, Greene,
and others: Then Mowbray in Ar-
mor, and Harrold.

Rich. Marſhall, demand of yonder Champion
The cauſe of his arrivall here in Armes,
Aske him his name, and orderly proceed
To ſweare him in the juſtice of his cauſe.
Mar. In Gods Name, and the Kings, ſay who thou art,
And why thou com'ſt, thus Knightly clad in Armes?
Againſt what man thou com'ſt, and what's thy quarrell,
Speake truely, on thy Knighthood, and thine oath,
As ſo defend thee heaven, and thy valour.
Mow. My name is *Tho. Mowbray,* Duke of Norfolke,
Who hither come engaged by my oath
(Which heaven defend a Knight ſhould violate)
Both to defend my loyalty and truth,
To God, my King, and his ſucceeding iſſue,
Ag ainſt the Duke of Hereford, that appeales me.

　　　　　　　B 2　　　　　　And

4

8

12

16

20

And by the grace of God and this mine arme,
To proue him (in defending of my felfe)
24 A traytor to my God, my King, and me,
And as I truely fight, defend me heauen.

Tucket.   Enter Hereford, and Harold.
Rich. Marfhall: aske yonder Knight in Armes,
Both who he is, and why he commeth hither,
28 Thus placed in habiliments of warre:
And formally according to our Law
Depofe him in the iuftice of his caufe.   (ther
Mar. What is thy name, and wherefore com'ft thou hi-
Before King *Richard* in his Royall Lifts ?
32 Againft whom com'ft thou? and what's thy quarrell?
Speake like a true Knight, fo defend thee Heauen.
† *Bul. Harry of Hereford, Lancaster,* and *Derby,*
36 Am I: who ready here doe ftand in Armes,
To prove by heauens grace, and my bodies valour,
In Lifts, on *Thomas Mowbray* Duke of Norfolke,
That he's a Traytor foule and dangerous,
40 To God of heauen, King *Richard,* and to me,
And as I truely fight, defend me heauen.
Mar. On paine of death, no perfon be fo bold,
Or daring hardy as to touch the Lifts,
44 Except the Marfhall, and fuch Officers
Appoynted to direct thefe faire defignes.
Bul. Lord Marfhall, let me kiffe my Soueraignes hand,
And bow my knee before his Maiefty:
48 For *Mowbray* and my felfe are like two men,
That vow a long and weary pilgrimage,
Then let vs take a ceremonius leaue
And loving farewell of our feuerall friends.
52 *Mar.* The Appealant in all duty greets your Highnes,
And craues to kiffe your hand, and take his leaue.
Rich. We will defcend, and fold him in our armes.
Cofin of *Hereford* as thy caufe is iuft,
56 So be thy fortune in this royall fight:
Farewell, my blood, which if to day thou fhead,

                                          Lament

Lament we may, but not reuenge thee dead.

Bul. Oh let no Noble eye prophane a teare
For me, if I be goar'd with *Morbrayes* fpeare: 60
As confident, as is the Falcons flight
Againft a Bird, doe I with *Mowbray* fight.
My loving Lord, I take my leave of you,
Of you (my Noble Cofin) Lord *Aumerle* ; 64
Not ficke, although I have to doe with death,
But lufty, young, and chearely drawing breath.
Loe, as at Englifh Feafts, fo I regreet
The daintieft laft, to make the end moft fweet. 68
Oh thou the earthy author of my blood,
Whofe youthfull fpirit in me regenerate,
Doth with a two-fold vigor lift me up
To reach at victory above my head, 72
Adde proofe unto mine Armour with thy prayers,
And with thy bleffings fteele my Lances-poynt,
That it may enter *Mowbayes* waxen Coate,
And furbifh new the name of *Iohn a Gaunt,* 76
Even in the lufty haviour of his fonne.

Gaunt. Heaven in thy good caufe make thee profp'rous,
Be fwift like lightning in the execution,
And let thy blowes doubly redoubled, 80
Fall like amazing thunder on the Caske
Of thy amaz'd pernicious enemy.
Rouze up thy youthfull blood, be valiant and live.

Bul. Mine innocence, and S. *George* to thrive. 84

Mow. How ever Heaven or fortune caft my lot,
There lives, or dyes, true to King *Richards* Throne,
A loyall, iuft, and upright Gentleman:
Never did Captiue with a freer heart, 88
Caft off his chaines of bondage, and embrace
His golden uncontroul'd enfranchifement,
More than my dancing foule doth celebrate
This Feaft of Battle, with mine adverfary. 92
Moft mighty Liege, and my companion Peeres,
Take from my mouth, the wifh of happy yeares,
As gentle, and as jocond, as to jeft,

B 3 Goe

96 Goe I to fight : Truth, hath a quiet breaſt.
   *Rich.*Farewell,my Lord, ſecurely I eſpie
Vertue with valour, couched in thine eye :
Order the tryall Marſhall, and begin.
100   *Mar.*-*Harry* of Hereford,Lancaſter,and Derby
Receive thy Lance,and heaven defend thy right.
   Bul. Strong as a Towre in hope, I cry; Amen.
   Mar. Goe beare this Lance to *Thomas* D.of Norfolke,
104   1 *Har. Harry* of Hereford,Lancaſter,and Derby,
Stands here for God, his Soveraigne,and himſelfe,
On paine to be found falſe and recreant,
To prove the Duke of Norfolke,*Thomas Mowbray,*
108 A Traytor to his God,his King, and him,
And dares him to ſet forwards to the fight.
   2. *Har.* Here ſtandeth *Tho, Mowbray* Duke of Norfolke
On paine to be found falſe and recreant,
112 Both to defend himſelfe,and to approve
Henry of Hereford,Lancaſter,and Derby,
To God,his Soveraigne, and to him diſloyall:
Couragiouſly, and with a free deſire,
116 Attending but the ſignall to begin.   *A charge ſounded.*
   *Mar.*Sound Trumpets,and ſet forward Combatants.
Stay,the King hath throwne his Warder downe.
   Rich. Let them lay by their Helmets and their Speares,
120 And both returne backe to their Chaires againe :
Withdraw with us,and let the Trumpets ſound,
While we returne theſe Dukes,what we decree,
        A long flouriſh.
124 Draw neere and liſt
What with our councell we have done.
For that our Kingdomes earth ſhould not be ſoyld
With that deare blood which it hath foſtered,
And for our eyes doe hate the dire aſpect
128 Of civill wounds plough'd up with neyghbours ſwords,
134 Which ſo rouz'd up with boyſtrous untun'd drummes,
With harſh reſounding Trumpets dreadfull bray,
And grating ſhocke of wrathfull yron Armes,
Might from our quiet Confines fright faire Peace,

                            And

of Richard *the second.*

And make us wade even in our kindreds blood: *138*
Therefore, we banish you our Territories.
You Cosin Hereford, upon paine of death,
Till twice five Summers have enrich'd our fields,   *142*
Shall not regreet our faire Dominions,
But tread the stranger paths of banishment.
  Bul. Your will be done: this must my comfort be,
That Sunne that warmes you here shall shine on me:
And those his golden beames to you here lent,   *146*
Shall poynt on me, and gilde my banishment.
  Rich. Norfolke: for thee remaines a heavier doome.
Which I with some unwillingnesse pronounce,
The flye slow houres shall not determinate   *150*
The datelesse limit of thy deare exile:
The hopelesse word, of never to returne,
Breathe against thee, upon paine of life.   †
  Mow. A heavy sentence my most Soveraigne Liege,   *154*
And all unlook'd for from your Highnesse mouth:
A deerer merit, not so deepe a maime,
As to be cast forth in the common ayre
Have I deserved at your Highnesse hands.   *158*
The Language I have learn'd these forty yeares
(My native English) now I must forgoe,
And now my tongues use is to me no more,
Then an unstringed Vyoll, or a Harpe,   *162*
Or like a cunning Instrument cas'd up,
Or being open, put into his hands
That knowes no touch to tune the harmony.
Within my mouth you have engaol'd my tongue   *166*
Doubly purcullist with my teeth and lips,   †
And dull, unfeeling, barren ignorance,
Is made my gaoler to attend on me:
I am too old to fawne upon a Nurse,   *170*
To farre in yeares to be a pupill now:
What is thy sentence then, but speechlesse death,
Which robs my tongue from breatheing native breath?
  Rich. It boots thee not to be compassionate,   *174*
After our sentence, plaining comes too late-

                        Mow.

The Life and Death

Mow. Then thus I turne me from my Countries light
To dwell in folemne fhades of endleſſe night.
Rich. Returne againe and take an oath with thee,
Lay on our royall Sword, your baniſht hands,
Sweare by the duty that you owe to heaven
(Our part therein we baniſh with your ſelves)
To kepe the Oath that we adminiſter :
You never fhall (ſo helpe you Truth and Heaven)
Embrace each others loue in baniſhment,
Nor ever looke upon each others face,
Nor ever writ, regreete, or reconcile
This lowring tempeſt of your home-bred hate,
Nor ever by adviſed purpoſe meet,
To plot, contrive, or complot any ill,
Gainſt Vs our State, our Subjeɕs, or our Land,
Bul. I ſweare.
Mow And I to keepe all this.
Bul. Norfolke, ſo farre, as to mine enemy,
By this time (had the King permitted us)
One of our ſoules had wandred in the ayre,
Baniſh'd this frayle ſepulcher of our fleſh,
As now our fleſh is baniſh'd from this Land.
Confeſſe thy Treaſons, ere thou flie this Realme,
Since thou haſt farre to goe, beare not along
The clogging burthen of a guilty ſoule.
Mow. No *Bullingbrooke*: If ever I were Traitor,
My name be blotted from the Booke of Life,
And I from heaven baniſh'd, as from hence :
But what thou art, heaven, thou, and I doe know,
And all too ſoone (I feare) the King fhall rue.
Farewell (my Liege) now no way can I ſtray,
Save backe to England, all the worlds my way.
Rich. Vncle, even in the glaſſes of thine eyes
I ſee thy grieved heart : thy ſad aſpeɕ,
Hath from the number of his baniſh'd yeares
Pluck'd foure away: ſixe frozen Winters ſpent,
Returne with welcome home from baniſhment.
Bul. How long a time lyes in one little word:

Foure

Foure lagging Winters, and foure wanton Springs   *214*
End in a word, ſuch is the breath of Kings.

    Gaunt. I thanke my Liege, that in regard of me
He ſhortens foure yeares of my ſonnes exile :
But little vantage ſhall I reape thereby.   *218*
For ere theſe ſixe yeares that he hath to ſpend   †
Can change the Moones, and bring their times about,
My oyle-dride Lampe, and time-bewaſted light
Shall be extinct with age, and endleſſe night :   *222*
My inch of Taper, will be burnt, and done,
And blindfold death, not let me ſee my ſonne.

    Rich. Why Vncle, thou haſt many yeares to live.

    Gaunt. But not a minute (King) that thou canſt give ;   *226*
Shorten my dayes thou canſt with ſudden ſorrow,
And plucke nights from me, but not lend a morrow :
Thou canſt helpe time to furrow me with age,
But ſtop no wrincle in his pilgrimage :   *230*
Thy word is currant with him, for my death,
But dead, thy kingdome cannot buy my breath.

    Rich. Thy ſonne is baniſh'd upon good aduice
Whereto thy tongue a party-verdict gave,   *234*
Why at our Iuſtice ſeem'ſt thou then to lowre?

    Gan. Things ſweet to taſt, prove in digeſtion ſowre :
You urg'd me as a Iudge, but I had rather
You would have bid me argue like a Father.   *238*
Alas, I look'd when ſome of you ſhould ſay,   *243*
I was too ſtrict to make mine owne away :
But you gave leave to my unwilling tongue,
Againſt my will, to do my ſelfe this wrong.   *246*

    Rich. Coſin farewell: and Vncle bid him ſo:
Six yeares we baniſh him, and he ſhall go.   *Exit.*

        Flouriſh.

    Au. Coſm farewell; what preſence muſt not know
From where you do remaine, let paper ſhow.   *250*

    Mar. My Lord, no leave take I, for I will ride
As farre as land will let me, by your ſide.

    Gaunt. Oh to what purpoſe doſt thou hord thy words,
That thou return'ſt no greeting to thy friends ?   *254*
        C   *Bul.*

The Life and Death

Bul. I haue too few to take my leaue of you,
When the tongues office should be prodigall,
To breath th' abundant dolour of the heart.

Gau. Thy griefe is but thy absence for a time.

Bul. Ioy absent, griefe is present for that time.

Gau. What is sixe Winters, they are quickly gone?

Bul. To men in ioy, but griefe makes one houre ten.

Gau, Call it a trauell, that thou takest for pleasure.

Bul. My heart will sigh, when I miscall it so,
Which finds it an inforced Pilgrimage.

Gaunt. The sullen passage of thy weary steps
Esteeme a soyle, wherein thou art to set
The precious Iewell of thy home returne.

Bul. Oh who can hold a fire in his hand
By thinking on the frosty *Caucasus?*
Or cloy the hungry edge of appetite,
By bare imagination of a feast?
Or wallow naked in December snow
By thinking on phantasticke Summers heate?
Oh no, the apprehension of the good
Giues but the greater feeling to the worse:
Fell sorrowes tooth, doth euer rankle more
Then when it bites, but lanceth not the sore.

Gau. Come, come (my sonne) Ile bring thee on thy way
Had I thy youth, and cause, I would not stay.

Bul. Then Englands ground farewell; sweet soyle adieu,
My Mother, and my Nurse, which beares me yet:
Where ere I wander, boast of this I can,
Though banish'd, yet a true-borne Englishman.

Scæna Quarta.

Enter King, Aumerle, Greene, and Bagot.
Rich. We did obserue. Cosin *Aumerle,*
How farre brought you high *Hereford* on his way.

Aum-

Aum. I brought high Hereford (if you call him so) 4
But to the next high way, and there I left him.

Rich. And say, what store of parting teares were shed ?

Aum. Faith none by me: except the Northeast wind
Which then blew bitterly against our face, 8 †
Awak'd the sleepy rhewme, and so by chance
Did grace our hollow parting with a teare.

Rich. What said our Cosin when you parted with him?

Au. Farewell: & for my heart disdained that my tongue 12
Should so prophane the word, that taught me craft
To counterfeit oppreßion of such griefe,
That word seem'd buried in my sorrowes grave.
Marry, would the word farewell, had lengthen'd houres, 16
And added yeeres to his short banishment,
He should have had a volume of Farewels,
But since it would not, he had none of me.

Rich. He is our Cosin (Cosin) but 'tis doubt, 20
When time shall call him home from banishment,
Whether our kinsman come to see his friends,
Our selfe, and *Bushy, Bagot* here and *Greene* †
Obseru'd his Courtship to the common people: 24
How he did seeme to dive into their hearts,
With humble, and familiar courtesie,
What reverence he did throw away on slaves;
Wooing poore Craftesmen, with the craft of smiles, 28
And patient under-bearing of his Fortune,
As 'twere to banish their affects with him.
Off goes his bonnet to an Oyster-wench,
A brace of Dray-men bid God speed him well, 32
And had the tribute of his supple knee,
With thankes my Countrimen, my Loving friends,
As were our England in reuersion his,
And he our subjects next degree in hope. 36

Gr. VVell, he is gone, and with him goe these thoughts
Now for the Rebels, which stand out in *Ireland*,
Expedient mannage must be made my Liege
Ere further leysure, yeeld the further meanes 40 †
For their aduantage, and your highneße loße.

The Life and Death

Rich. We will our felfe in perfon to this warre,
And for our Coffers, with too great a Court,
And liberall Largeffe, are growne fomewhat light,
We are enforc'd to farme our royall Realme,
The revenew whereof fhall furnifh us
For our affaires in hand : if they come fhort.
Our fubftitutes at home fhall have Blancke-charters :
Whereto, when they fhall know what men are rich,
They fhall fubfcribe them for large fummes of Gold,
And fend them after to fupply our wants:
For we will make for Ireland prefently.
                    Enter Bufhy.
Bufhy, what newes ?
    Bu. Old *Iohn a Gaunt* is very ficke my Lord,
Sodainely taken, and hath fent poft hafte
To entreat your Maiefty to vifite him.
    Rich. Where lyes he ?
    Bu. At Ely-houfe.
    Rich. Now put it (heaven) in his Phyfitians mind,
To helpe him to his grave immediately:
The linning of his coffers fhall make Coates
To decke our Souldiers for thefe Irifh warres.
Come Gentlemen, let's all go vifit him :
Pray heaven we may make hafte, and come too late, *Exit.*

Actus Secundus, Scæna Prima.

Enter Gaunt ficke, with the Duke of Torke.

Gau. Will the King come, that I may breath my laft
In wholfome counfell to his unftayd youth?
    Tor. Vex not your felfe, nor ftrive not with your breath
For all in vaine comes counfell to his eare
    Gau. Oh but (they fay) the tongues of dying men
Inforce attention, like deepe harmony;
                                        Where

Where words are scarse, they are seldome spent in vaine,
For they breath truth, that breath their words in paine. 8
He that no more must say, is listen'd more
Then they whom youth and ease have taught to glose,
More are mens ends mark'd, then their lives before,
The setting Sunne, and musicke is the close 12
As the last taste of sweetes, is sweetest last,
Writ in remembrance, more then things long past :
Though *Richard* my lives counsell would not heare,
My deaths sad tale, may yet un-deafe his eare. 16
  Yor. No, it is stopt with other flatt'ring sounds
As prayses of his state : then there are found
Lacivious Meeters, to whose venome sound
The open eares of youth doth alwaies listen. 20
Report of fashions in proud Italy,
Whose manners still our tardy apish Nation
Limpes after in base imitation.
Where doth the world thrust forth a vanity, 24
So it be new, there's no respect how vile,
That is not quickly buzz'd into their eares ?
That all too late comes counsell to be heard,
Where will doth mutiny with wits regard : 28
Direct not him, whose way himselfe will chose,
Tis breath thou lackst, and that breath wilt thou loose
  Gaunt. Me thinkes I am a Prophet new inspir'd,
And thus expiring doe foretell of him, 32
His rash fierce blaze of Ryot cannot last,
For violent fires soone burne out themselues ;
Small shoures last long, but sodaine stormes are short,
He tyres betimes, that spurs too fast betimes ; 36
With eager feeding food doth choake the feeder ;
Light vanity, insatiat cormorant,
Consuming meanes soone preyes upon it selfe. †
This royall Throne of Kings, this Sceptred Isle, 40
This earth of Majesty, this seate of Mars ,
This other Eden, demy Paradise,
This Fortres built by nature for her selfe,
Against infection, and the hand of warre: 44
                                        This

C 3

The Life and Death

This happy breed of men, this little world,
This precious ſtone ſet in the ſilver Sea,
VVhich ſerves it in the office of a wall,
Or as a Moate defenſiue to a houſe,
Againſt the enuy of leſſe happier Lands,
This bleſſed plot, this Earth this Realme, this England,
This Nurſe, this teeming wombe of Royall Kings,
Fear'd by their breed, and famous for their birth,
Renowned for their deeds, as farre from home,
For Chriſtian ſervice and true Chivalry,
As is the ſepulcher in ſtubborne *Iury*
Of the worlds ranſome, bleſſed *Maries* ſonne.
This Land of ſuch deare ſoules, this deare deare Land,
Deare for her reputation through the world,
Is now Leas'd out (I dye pronouncing it)
Like to a Tenement, or pelting Farme.
England bound in with the triumphant Sea,
VVhoſe rocky ſhore beates backe the envious ſiedge
Of watry Neptune, is now bound in with ſhame,
VVith Inky blottes, and rotten Parchment bonds.
That England that was wont to conquer others,
Hath made a ſhamefull conqueſt of it ſelfe.
Ah, would the ſcandall vaniſh with my life,
How happy then were my enſuing death?

Enter King, Queene, Aumerle, Buſhy, Greene,
Bagot, Ros, and Willoughby.

Tor. The King is come, deale mildly with his youth,
For young hot Coalts, being rag'd, doe rage the more.
Qu. How fares our noble Vncle, *Lancaſter*?
Ri. VVhat comfort man? How iſt with aged *Gaunt*?
Ga. Oh how that name befits my compoſition:
Old *Gaunt* indeed, and gaunt in being old:
VVithin me griefe hath kept a teadious faſt,
And who abſtaines from meate, that is not gaunt:
For ſleeping England long time have I watcht
VVatching breeds leanneſſe, leanneſſe is all gaunt:
The pleaſure that ſome Fathers feed upon,

of Richard *the second.*

Is my ſtrict faſt, I meane my Childrens lookes,   80
And therein faſting, haſt thou made me gaunt :
Gaunt am I for the grave, gaunt as a grave,
VVhoſe hollow wombe inherits nought but bones.
   Rich. Can ſicke men play ſo nicely with their names ?   84
   Gau. No, miſery makes ſport to mocke it ſelfe :
Since thou doſt ſeeke to kill my name in me,
I mocke my name (great King) to flatter thee.
   Ric. Should dying men flatter thoſe that live?   88
   Gau. No,no, man living flatter thoſe that dye.
   Ric. Thou now a dying, ſayſt thou flatter'ſt me.
   Gau. O no, thou dyeſt, though I the ſicker be.
   Rich. I am in health I breathe, I ſee thee ill.   92
   Gau. Now he that made me, knowes I ſee thee ill:
Ill in my ſelfe to ſee, and in thee, ſeeing ill,
Thy death-bed is no leſſer then the Land,
VVherein thou lyeſt in reputation ſicke,   96
And thou too careleſſe patient as thou art.
Commit'ſt thy annoynted body to the cure
Of thoſe Phyſitions, that firſt wounded thee :
A thouſand flatterers ſit within thy Crowne,   100
VVhoſe compaſſe is no bigger then thy hand,
And yet encaged in ſo ſmall a Verge,   †
The waſte is no whit leſſer then thy Land,
Oh had thy Grandſir with a Prophets eye,   104
Seene how his ſonnes ſonne, ſhould deſtroy his ſonnes,
From forth thy reach he would have layd thy ſhame,
Depoſing thee before thou wert poſſeſt,
VVhich art poſſeſt now to depoſe thy ſelfe,   108
Why (Coſin) were thou Regent of the world,
It were a ſhame to let this Land by leaſe:
But for thy world enioying but this Land,
Is it not more then ſhame, to ſhame it ſo ?   112
Landlord of England art thou, and not King:
Thy ſtate of Law, is bondſlave to the Law,
And _____
   Rich. And thou, a lunaticke leane-witted foole,
Preſuming on an Agues privelledge.   116

                       Dar'ſt

Dar'ft with thy frozen admonition
Make pale our cheeke, chafing the Royall blood
With fury, from his native refidence?

120 Now by my Seates right Royall Maiefty,
Wert thou not brother to great *Edwards* fonne,
This tongue that runnes fo roundly in thy head,
Should runne thy head from thy unreverent fhoulders.

124 *Gau.* Oh fpare me not, my brother *Edwards* fonne,
For that I was his father *Edwards* fonne :
That blood already (like the Pellican)
Thou haft tapt out, and drunkenly carows'd.

128 My brother *Glocefter*, plaine well meaning foule,
(Whom faire befall in heaven 'mongft happy foules)
May be a prefident, and witneffe good,
That thou refpect'ft not fpilling *Edwards* blood :

132 Ioyne with the prefent fickeneffe that I haue,
And thy unkindneffe be like crooked age,
To crop at once a too-long wither'd flowre.
Live in thy fhame, but dye not fhame with thee,

136 Thefe words hereafter, thy tormentors be.
Convey me to my bed, then to my grave.
Love they to live, that love and honour have.   *Exit.*
Rich. And let them dye, that age and fullens have,

140 For both haft thou, and both become the grave.
Yor. I doe befeech your Maiefty impute his words
To wayward ficklineffe, and age in him :
He loues you on my life, and holds you deare

144 As *Harry* Duke of *Hereford*, were he here.
Rich. Right, you fay true : as *Herefords* love, fo his ;
As theirs, fo mine : and all be as it is.

Enter Northumberland.

Nor. My Liege, old *Gaunt* commends him to your
Maiefty.
Rich. What fayes he ?

148 *Nor.* Nay nothing, all is fayd :
His tongue is now a ftringleffe inftrument.
Words, life, and all, old *Lancafter* hath fpent.

Yor.

Yor. Be Yorke the next,that muſt be bankrupt ſo,
Though death be poore, it ends a mortall wo.   152
 *Rich.*The ripeſt fruit firſt fals, and ſo doth he,
His time is ſpent, our pilgrimage muſt be :
So much for that. Now for our Iriſh warres,
We muſt ſupplant thoſe rough rug-headed Kernes,   156
Which live like venom, where no venom elſe
But onely they have privelledge to live.
And for theſe great affaires do aske ſome charge
Towards our aſſiſtance, we doe ſeize to us   160
The plate,coyne,and revennews, and moveables,
Whereof our Vncle *Gaunt* did ſtand poſſeſt,
 Yor. How long ſhall I be patient ? Oh how long
Shall tender duty make me ſuffer wrong ?   164
Not *Gloſters* death, nor *Herefords* baniſhment,
Nor *Gaunts* rebukes,nor Englands private wrongs,
Nor the prevention of poore *Bullingbrooke,*
About his marriage, nor my owne diſgrace   168
Have ever made me ſowre my patient cheeke,
Or bend one wrinkle on my ſoveraignes face :
I am the laſt of noble *Edwards* ſonnes,
Of whom thy father Prince of Wales was firſt :   172
In warres was never Lyon rag'd more fierce :
In peace, was never gentle Lambe more mild,
Then was that young and Princely Gentleman:
His face thou haſt,for even ſo look'd he   176
Accompliſh'd with the number of thy howers :
But when he frown'd, it was againſt the French,
And not againſt his friends : his noble hand
Did win what he did ſpend : and ſpent not that   180
Which his triumphant fathers hand had won :
His hands were guilty of no kindreds blood,
But bloody with the enemies of his kinne :
Oh *Richard, Yorke* is too farre gone with griefe,   184
Or elſe he never would compare betweene.
 Rich. Why Vncle,
What's the matter ?
 Yor. Oh my Liege, pardon me if you pleaſe, if not
        D   I

The Life and Death

188 | I pleas'd not to be pardon'd, am content with all:
Seeke you to feize, and gripe into your hands
The Royalties and Rightes of banifh'd *Hereford*?
Is not *Gaunt* dead? and doth not *Hereford* live?
192 | Was not *Gaunt* juft? and is not *Harry* true ?
Did not the one deferve to have an heyre ?
Is not his heyre a well-deferving fonne?
Take *Herefords* rights away, and take from time
196 | His Charters, and his cuftom rie rights :
Let not to morrow then infue to day,
Be not thy felfe. For how art thou a King
But by faire fequence and fucceffion ?
200 | Now afore God, God forbid I fay true,
If you doe wrongfully feize *Herefords* right,
Call in his Letters Patents that he hath
By his Atturneyes generall, to fue
204 | His Livery, and deny his offer'd homage,
You plucke a thoufand dangers on your head,
You loofe a thoufand well-difpofed hearts,
And pricke my tender patience to thofe thoughts
208 | Which honor and allegeance cannot thinke.
       Ric. Thinke what you will : we feife into our hands,
His plate, his goods, his money, and his lands.
       Yor. Ile not be by the while : My Leige farewell,
212 | What will enfue hereof, there's none can tell,
But by bad courfes may be underftood.
That their events can never fall out good.   *Exit.*
       Rich. Goe *Bufhie* to the Earle of *Wiltfhire* ftreight,
216 | Bid him repaire to us to *Ely* Houfe,
To fee this bufineffe : to morrow next
We will for *Ireland*, and 'tis time, I trow:
And we create in abfence of our felfe
220 | Our Vnckle *Yorke*, Lord Governer of England :
For he is juft, and alwayes lov'd us well.
Come on our Queene, to morrow muft we part,
Be merry, for our time of ftay is fhort.   *Flourifh.*
       Manet North Willonghby, and Roff.
224 | *Nor.* Well Lords, the Duke of Lancafter is dead.
                                                    Roff.

Roff. And living too,for now his fonne is Duke.

Will. Barely in title, not in revennew.

Nor. Richly in both , if juftice had her right.

Roff. My heart is great : but it muft breake with filence   228
Eer't be disburthen'd'with a liberall tongue.

Nor. Nay fpeake thy mind & let him ne'r fpeake more
That fpeakes thy words againe to doe thee harme.

Wil. Tends that thou'd ft fpeake to th' D. of Hereford?   232 ↓
If it be fo,out with it boldly man:
Quicke is mine eare to heare of good towards him.

Roff. No good at all that I can doe for him,
Vnleffe you call it good to pity him,   236
Bereft and gelded of his patrimony.

Nor. Now afore heaven , 'ts fhame fuch wrongs are   †
borne,
In him a royall Prince, and many moe
Of noble blood in this declintng Land;   240
The King is not himfelfe, but bafely led
By flatterers, and what they will informe
Meerely in hate 'gainft any of us all:
That will the King feverely profecute·   244
'Gainft us,our lives, our children,and our heires.

Roff. The Commons hath he pill'd with grievous taxes
And quite loft their hearts: the Nobles hath he fin'd
For ancient quarrels,and quite loft their hearts.   248

Wil. And daily new exactions are devis'd,
As blankes,benevolences, and I wot not what:
But what o' Gods name doth become of this ?

Nor. Warres hath not wafted it,for warr'd he hath not,   252
But bafely yeelded upon comprimize,
That which his Anceftors atchieu'd with blowes:
More hath he fpent in peace,then they in warres.

Roff. The Earle of Wiltfhire hath the Realme in farme.   256

Wil. The King's growne bankrupt like a broken man.

Nor. Reproach,and defolution hangeth over him.

Roff. He hath not money for thefe Irifh warres:
(His burthenous taxations notwithftanding)   260
But by the robbing of the banifh'd Duke.

Nor.

II.i.

Nor. His noble Kinſman, moſt degenerate King:
But Lords,we heare this fearefull tempeſt ſing
264   Yet ſeeke no ſhelter to avoyd the ſtorme:
We ſee the winde ſit ſore upon our ſailes,
And yet we ſtrike not,but ſecurely periſh,
   *Roſ.*We ſee the uery wracke that we muſt ſuffer,
268   And unavoyded is the danger now
For ſuffering ſo the cauſes of our wracke.
   *Nor.*Not ſo; even through the hollow eyes of death,
†   I ſpie life peercing: but I dare not ſay,
272   How neere the tidings of our comfort is.
   Wil Nay,let us ſhare thy thoughts,as thou doſt ours.
   *Roſ.*Be confident to ſpeake Northumberland,
We three,are but thy ſelfe, and ſpeaking ſo,
276   Thy words are but as thoughts, therefore be bold.
   Nor. Then thus: I have from Port *le Blan*
A Bay in *Britaine*, receiv'd intelligence,
†   That *Harry* Duke of *Hereford*, *Raynald* Lord *Cobham*,
281   That late broke from the Duke of *Exeter*,
His brother Archbiſhop, late of *Canterbury*,
Sir *Thomas Erpingham*, Sir *Iohn Rainſton*,
284   Sir *Iohn Norbery*,Sir *Robert Waterton*,and *Francis Quoint*,
All theſe well furniſh'd by the Duke of *Brittaine*,
With eight tall ſhips,three thouſand men of warre
Are making hither with all due expedience,
288   And ſhortly meane to touch our Northerne ſhore:
Perhaps they had ere this, but that they ſtay
The firſt departing of the King for Ireland.
If then we ſhall ſhake off our ſlaviſh yoake,
†292   Iumpe out our drooping Countries broken wing,
Redeeme from broken pawne, the blemiſh'd Crowne,
†   Wipe off the duſt that hides the Scepters gilt,
And make high Majeſty looke like it ſelfe,
296   Away with me in poſte to *Ravenſpurgh*,
But if you faint, as fearing to doe ſo,
Stay and be ſecret and my ſelfe will goe.
   *Roſ.*To horſe, to horſe,urge doubts to them that feare.
300   *Wil.* Hold out my horſe,and I will firſt be there, *Exeu.*
                             Scena

Scena Sæcunda.

Enter Queene, Bushy, and Bagot.
Bush. Madam, your Majesty is too much sad,
You promis'd when you parted with the King,
To lay aside selfe-harming heavinesse,
And entertaine a cheerefull disposition.   4

   Qu. To please the King, I did : to please my selfe
I cannot doe it : yet I know no cause
Why I should welcome such a guest as griefe,
Save bidding farewell to so sweet a guest   8
As my sweet *Richard* , yet againe me thinkes
Some unborne sorrow ripe in fortunes wombe
Is comming towards me , and my inward soule
With nothing trembles, at something it grieves,   12
More than with parting from my Lord the King.

   Bush. Each substance of a griefe had twenty shadows   †
Which shewes like griefe it selfe, but is not so:
For sorrowes eye glazed with blinding teares,   16
Divides one thing intire, to many objects
Like perspectives, which rightly gaz'd upon
Shew nothing but confusion, ey'd awry,
Distinguisht forme: so your sweet Maiesty   20†
Looking awry upon your Lords departure,
Find shapes of griefe, more then himselfe to waile,
Which look'd on as it is, is nought but shadowes
Of what it is not, then thrice-gracious Queene,   24
More then your Lords departure weepe not, more's not
Or if it be, tis with false sorrows eye,   (seene;
Which for things true, weepe things imaginary.

   Qu. It may be so, but yet my inward soule   28
Perswades me it is otherwise how ere it be,
I cannot but be sad : so heavy sad.

        D 3   As

As though on thinking on no thought I thinke,
Makes me with heavy nothing faint and fhrinke.
Bufh. 'Tis nothing but conceit (my gracious Lady.)
Qu.'Tis nothing leffe : conceit is ftill deriu'd
From fome fore father greefe, mine is not fo,
For nothing hath begot my fomething griefe,
Orfomething, hath the nothing that I grieve,
'Tis in reverfion that I doe poffeffe,
But what it is,that is not yet knowne, what
I cannot name, 'tis namelefle woe I wot.   *Enter Green.*
  Gree. Heaven fave your Majefty,and well met Gentle-
I hope the King is not yet fhipt for Ireland.   (men;
  Qu. Why hop'ft thou fo?'Tis better hope he is :
For his defignes crave hafte, good hope,
Then wherefore doft thou hope he is not fhipt ?
  Gree. That he our hope, might have retyr'd his power,
And driven into defpaire an enemies hope,
Who ftrongly hath fet footing in this Land,
The banifh'd *Bullingbrooke* repeales himfelfe,
And with up-lifted Armes is fafe arriu'd
At *Rauenfpurg.*
  Qu. Now God in heaven forbid.
  Gree. O Maddam 'tis too true: and that is worfe,
The L. Northumberland, his young fonne,*Henry Percy,*
The Lords of Rolfe,*Beaumond,*and *Willoughby.*
With all their powerfull friends are fled to him.
  Bufh. Why have you not proclaim'd Northumberland
And the reft of the revolted faction, Traytors ?
  Gree. We have : whereupon the Earle of Worcefter
Hath broke his ftaffe,refign'd his Stewardfhip, (*brook*
And all the houfhold feruants fled with him to *Bullen.*
  Qu. So *Greene,* thou art the Midwife of my woe,
And *Bullingbrooke* my forrowes difmall heyre :
Now hath my foule brought forth her prodigy,
And I a gafping new delivered mother,
Haue woe to woe, forrow to forrow ioyn'd.
  Bufh. Defpaire not Madam.
  Qu. Who fhall hinder me ?

                                              I will

of Richard *the second.*

I will defpaire, and be at emnity

With couzening hope ; he is a flatterer,

A Parafite, a keeper backe of death,

Who gently would diffolve the bands of life,

Which falfe hopes linger in extremity.

Enter Yorke.

Gree. Here comes the Duke of Yorke.

Qu. With figenes of warre about his aged necke,

Oh full of carefull bufineffe are his lookes :

Vncle, for heavens fake fpeake comfortable words.

Yor. Comfort's in Heaven, and we are on the earth,.

Where nothing lives but croffes, care, and griefe :

Your husband he is gone to fave farre off,

Whilft others come to make his loofe at home :

Here am I left to underprop his Land,

Who weake with age, cannot fupport my felfe :

Now comes his ficke houre that his furfeit made,

Now fhall he try his friends that flattered him.

Enter a Servant.

Ser. My Lord, your fonne was gone before I came.

Yor. He was : why fo, goe all which way it will :

The Nobles they are fled, the Commons they are cold,

And will I feare revolt on *Herefords* fide.

Sirra, get thee to Plafhy to my fifter *Glofter,*

Bid her fend me prefently a thoufand pound,

Hold, take my Ring.

Ser. My Lord, I had forgot

To tell your Lordfhip, to day I came by, and call'd there,

But I fhall grieve you to report the reft.

Yor. What is't knave ?

Ser. An houre before I came, the Dutcheffe di'de.

Yo. Heaven for his mercy, what a tide of woes

Come rufhing on this wofull Land at once ?

I know not what to doe : I would to heaven

(So my vntruth hath not provok'd him to it)

The King had cut off my head with my brothers.

What, are there poftes difpatcht for Ireland ?

How fhall we doe for money for thefe warres ?

Com.

Come fifter (Cofin I would fay) pray pardon me.
Goe fellow, get thee home, provide fome Carts,
And bring away the Armour that is there.
108   Gentlemen, will you mufter men?
If I know how, or which way to order thefe affaires
Thus diforderly thruft into my hands.
Never beleeve me. Both are my kinfmen,
112   Th'one is my Soveraigne, whom both my oath
†   And duty bids defend: the other againe
Is my kinfman, whom the King hath wrong'd,
Whom confcience, and my kindred bids to right,
116   Well, fomewhat we muft doe: Come Cofin,
Ile difpofe of you, Gentlemen, goe mufter up your men,
And meet me prefently at Barkley Caftle:
120   I fhould to Plafhy too, but time will not permit,
†   All is uneven, and every thing is left at fix and feven. *Ex.*
      Bufh. The wind fits faire for newes to goe to Ireland,
124   But none returnes: for us to levy power
Proportionable to th'enemy, is all impoffible.
      Gree. Befides our neereneffe to the King in love,
128   Is neere the hate of thofe love not the King.
      Bag. And that's the wavering Commons, for their love
†   Lies in their purfes, and whofo empties them,
By fo much fils their hearts with deadly hate.
†132   *Bufh.* Therein the King ftands generally condemn'd.
      Bag. If judgement lye in them, then fo doe we,
Becaufe we have beene ever neere the King.
      Gree. Well: I will for refuge ftreight to Briftoll Caftle,
136   The Earle of Wiltfhire is already there.
      Bufh. Thither will I with you, for little office
Will the hatefull Commons performe for us,
Except like Curres, to teare us all in pieces:
140   Will you goe along with us?
      Bag. No, I will to Ireland to his Maiefty:
Farewell, if hearts prefages be not vaine,
†   We three here part, that nev'r fhall meete againe.
144   *Bu.* That's as *Yorke* thrives to beate backe *Bullinbrooke*.
      Gr. Alas poore Duke, the taske he undertakes

                                              Is

of Richard *the second.*

Is numbring sands, and drinking Oceans dry,
Where one on his side fights, thousands will flye.
  Bush. Farewell at once, for once, for all, and ever.
Well, we may meet againe.
  Bag. I feare me never.   *Exit.*

Scæna Tertia.

Enter the Duke of Hereford, and Northum-
berland.

  Bul. How farre is it my Lord to Barkley now?
  Nor. Beleeve me noble Lord,
I am a stranger here in *Glostershire.*
These high wide hils, and rough uneven wayes; 4
Drawes out our miles, and makes them wearysome:
And yet our faire discourse hath beene as Sugar,
Making the hard way sweet and delectable:
But I bethinke me, what a weary way 8
From Ravenspurgh to Cottshold will be found,
In *Rosse* and *Willoughby,* wanting your company
Which I protest hath very much beguild
The teadiousnesse, and processe of my travell: 12
But theirs is sweetned with the hope to have
The present benefit that I possesse:
And hope to joy, is little lesse in joy,
Then hope enjoy'd: By this, the weary Lords 16
Shall make their way seeme short, as mine hath done,
By sight of what I have, your Noble company,
  Bul. Of much lesse valew is my company
Then your good words: but who comes here? 20
              Enter H. Percy.
  Nor. It is my sonne, young *Harry Percy,*
Sent from my brother *Worcester:* whencesoever,
Harry how fares your Vncle?   1
              E

                              Percy

Percy. I had thought, my Lord, to have learn'd his health of you.

Nor. Why is he not with the Queene?

Percy. No, my good Lord, he hath forſooke the Court, Broken his Staffe of Office, and diſperſt The Houſhold of the King.

Nor. What was his reaſon?
He was not ſo reſolv'd, when we laſt ſpake together.

Percy. Becauſe your Lordſhip was proclaimed Traytor. But he, my Lord, is gone to Ravenſpurgh, To offer ſervice to the Duke of Hereford, And ſent me over by Barkely, to diſcover What power the Duke of Yorke had levied there, Then with direction to repaire to Ravenſpurgh.

Nor. Have you forgot the Duke of Hereford (Boy?)

Percy. No, my good Lord ; for that is not forgot Which ne're I did remember: to my knowledge, I never in my life did looke on him.

Nor Then learne to know him now : this is the Duke.

Percy My gracious Lord, I tender you my ſervice, Such as it is, being tender, raw, and young, Which elder dayes ſhall ripen, and confirme To more approved ſervice and deſert.

But I thanke thee gentle *Percy,* and be ſure I count my elfe in nothing elſe ſo happy, As in a ſoule remembring my good friends: And as my fortune ripens with my love, It ſhall be ſtill thy true loves recompence, My heart this covenant makes, my hand thus ſeales it.

Nor How farre is it to Barkley ? and what ſtirre Keepes good old *Yorke* there, with his men of warre ?

Percy. There ſtands the Caſtle, by yond tuft of Trees, Mann'd with three hundred men, as I have heard, And in it are the Lords of *Yorke,* *Barkely,* and *Seymor,* None elſe of Name, and noble eſtimate.

Enter Roſſe, and Willoughby.
Nor. Here comes the Lords of *Roſſe,* and *Willoughby,*
Bloody

of Richard the second.

Bloody with spurring, fiery red with hast.

Bul. Welcome my Lords, I wot your love pursues
A banisht Traytor; all my Treasury   60
Is yet but unfelt thankes, which more enrich'd,
Shall be your love, and labours recompence.

Ros. Your presence makes vs rich, most Noble Lord.

Wil. And farre surmounts our labour to attaine it,   64

Bul. Evermore thankes, th'Exchequer of the poore,
Which till my infant-fortune comes to yeares,
Stands for my bounty : but who comes here?

Enter Barkely.

Nor. It is my Lord of *Barkely* as I guesse.   68

Bark. My Lord of Hereford, my message is to you.

Bul. My Lord, my answer is to *Lancaster*,
And I am come to seeke that name in England,
And I must find that Title in your Towne,   72
Before I make reply to ought you say.

Bark. Mistake me not, my Lord,'tis not my meaning
To raze one title of your honour out.
To you, my Lord, I come (what Lord you will)   76
From the most glorious of this Land,
The Duke of *Yorke*, to know what pricks you on
To take advantage of the absent time,
And fright our native peace with selfe-borne Armes.   80

Enter Yorke.

Bul. I shall not need transport my words by you,
Here comes his Grace in person.   My Noble Vncle.

Yor. Shew me thy humble Heart, and not thy Knee,
Whose duty is deceivable and false,   84

Bul. My gracious Vncle.

Yor. Tut, tut, Grace me no Grace, nor Vncle me,
I am no Traytors Vncle; and that word Grace,   88
In an ungracious mouth, is but prophane
Why have these banish'd, and forbidden Legges,
Dar'd once to touch the dust of Englands Ground?   †
But more then why, why have they dar'd to march   92
So many miles upon her peacefull Bosome,
Frighting her pale fac'd Villages with Warre,

E 2   And

And oftentation of defpifed Armes?
Com'ft thou becaufe th'anoynted King is hence?
Why foolifh Boy, the King is left behind,
And in my loyall Bofome lyes his power.
Were I but now the Lord of fuch hot youth,
As when braue *Gaunt* thy Father, and thy felfe,
Refcued the *blacke Prince*, that young *Mars* of men,
From forth the Rankes of many thoufand French:
Oh then, how quickly fhould this Arme of mine,
Now prifoner to the Plafhy, chaftife thee,
And minifter correction to thy fault.

    Bul. My gracious Vncle, let me know my fault,
On what condition ftands it, and wherein?

    Tor. Even in condition of the worft degree,
In groffe Rebellion, and detefted Treafon:
Thou art a banifh'd man, and here art come
Before th' expiration of thy time,
In braving Armes againft thy Soveraigne.

    Bul. As I was banifh'd, I was banifh'd *Hereford*,
But as a I come, I come for *Lancafter*.
And noble Vncle, I befeech your Grace
Looke on my wrongs with an indifferent eye:
You are my Father, for me thinkes in you
I fee old *Gaunt* alive. Oh then my Father,
Will you permit, that I fhall ftand condemn'd
A wandring Vagabond, my Rights and Royalties
Pluckt from my armes perforce, and given away
To upftart unthrifts? Wherefore was I borne?
If that my Coufin King, be King of England,
It muft be granted, I am Duke of Lancafter.
You have a fonne, *Aumerle*, my Noble Kinfman,
Had you firft died, and he bin thus trod downe,
He fhould have found his Vncle *Gaunt* a father,
To rowze his wrongs, and chafe them to the bay.
I am denyde to fue my Livery here,
And yet my Letters Pattens give me leave;
My fathers goods are all diftraynd, and fold
And thefe, and all amiffe imploy'd.

                                    What

of Richard *the second.*

What would you have me doe? I am a fubiect,
And challenge Law, Attorneyes are denyd me,
And therefore perfonally I lay my claime
To mine inheritance of free Defcent. 136
   Nor. The Noble Duke hath beene too much abus'd.
   Rof. It ftands your Grace upon to doe him right,
   Wil. Bafe men by his endowments are made great.
   Tor. My Lords of England, let me tell you this, 140
I have had feeling of my Cofins wrongs,
And labour'd all I could to doe him right :
But in this kind, to come in braving Armes,
Be his owne Carver, and cut out his way, 144
To find out Right with wrongs, it may not be;
And you that doe abeit him in this kind, †
Cherifh Rebellion, and are Rebels all.
   Tor. The Noble Duke hath fworne his comming is 148 †
But for his owne, and for the right of that,
We all have ftrongly fworne to give him ayd,
And let him nev'r fee joy, that breaks that oath.
   Tor. Well, well, I fee the iffue of thefe Armes, 152
I cannot mend it, I muft needs confeffe,
Becaufe my power is weake, and all ill left :
But if I could, by him that gave me life,
I would attach you all, and make you ftoope 156
Vnto the Soveraigne mercy of the King.
But fince I cannot, be it knowne to you,
I doe remaine as Neuter. So fare you well,
Vnleffe you pleafe to enter in the Caftle, 160
And there repofe you for this Night.
   Bul. An offer Vncle, that we will accept:
But we muft winne your Grace to goe with us
To Briftoll Caftle, which they fay is held 164 †
By *Bufhie, Bagot,* and their Complices,
The Caterpillers of the Commonwealth,
Which I have fworne to weede, and pluke away.
   Tor. It may be I will goe with you, but yet ile pawfe, 168
For I am loth to breake our Countries Lawes :
Not Friends, nor Foes, to me welcome you are, †

Things

The Life and Death

Things past redresse, are now with me past care. *Exeunt*

Scæna Quarta.

Enter Salisbury and a Captaine.

Capt. My Lord of Salisbury, we have stayd ten dayes,
And hardly kept our Countrymen together,
And yet we heare no tidings from the King:
Therefore we will disperse our selves: farewell.

Sal. Stay yet another day, thou trusty Welchman,
The King reposeth all his confidence in thee.

Capt. Tis thought the King is dead, we will not stay;
The Bay-trees in our Country all are wither'd,
The Meteors fright the fixed Starres of Heaven;
The pale-fac'd Moone lookes bloody on the Earth,
And leane-lookt Prophets whisper fearefull change;
Rich men looke sad, and Ruffians dance and leape,
The one in feare, to lose what they enioy,
The other to enjoy by Rage, and Warre:
These signes fore-run the death of Kings.
Farewell, our Countrymen are gone and fled,
As well assur'd *Richard* their King is dead.   *Exit.*

Sal. Ah *Richard*, with eyes of heauy mind,
I see thy Glory, like a shooting Starre,
Fall to the base Earth, from the Firmament:
Thy Sunne sets weeping in the lowly West.
Witnessing stormes to come, woe, and unrest:
Thy friends are fled, to waite upon thy foes,
And crossely to thy good, all fortune goes.   *Exit.*

Actus

Actus Tertius, Scæna Prima.

Enter Bullingbrooke, Yorke, Northumberland,
Roſſe, Percy, Willoughby; with Buſhy
and Greene, priſoners.

Bul. Bring forth theſe men :
Buſhy and *Greene*, I will not vex your ſoules,
(Since preſently your ſoules muſt part your bodies)
VVith two much urging your pernitious liues,   4
For twere no Charity : yet to waſh your blood
From off my hands, here in the view of men,
I will unfold ſome cauſes of your deaths,
You have miſ-led a Prince, a royall King,   8
A happy Gentleman in Blood, and Lineaments,
By you unhappied, and disfigur'd cleane :
You have in manner with your ſinfull houres
Made a Divorce betwixt his Queene and him,   12
Broke the Poſſeſſion of a Royall Bed,
And ſtayn'd the beauty of a faire Queenes Cheekes,
VVith teares drawne from her eyes, with your foule
My ſelfe a Prince, by fortune of my birth,   (wrongs.   16
Neere to the King in Blood, and neere in love,
Till you did make him miſ-interpret me,
Have ſtoopt my necke under your iniuries,
And ſigh'd my Engliſh breath in forraigne Clouds,   20
Eating the bitter bread of baniſhment;
VVhile you have fed upon my Seigniories,
Diſ-park'd my Parkes, and fell'd my Forreſt woods ;
From mine owne windowes torne my Houſhold Coat,   24
Raz'd 'out my Impreſe leaving me no ſigne,   †
Save mens opinions, and my living blood,
To ſhew the world I am a Gentleman.
This, and much more, much more then twice all this,   Con-   28

Condemnes you to the death: fee them delivered over
To execution, and the hand of death.

>32 *Bush.* More welcome is the ftroke ot death to me,
Then *Bullingbrooke* to England.

Gree. My comfort is, that Heaven will take onr foules,
And plague iniuftice with the paines of hell.

36 *Bul.* My Lord *Northumberland*, fee them difpatch'd:
Vncle, you fay the Queene is at your Houfe,
For Heavens fake, fairely let her be intreated,
Tell her, I fend to her my kind commends,
Take fpeciall care my greetings be deliver'd.

40 *Tor.* A Gentleman of mine, I have difpatch'd
VVith Letters of your loue to her at large.

Bul. Thankes gentle Vncle: come Lords away,
To fight with *Gendoure*, and his Complices;

†
44 A while to worke, and after holliday. *Exunt*

III.ii.

Scæna Secunda.

Drums, Flourifh, and Colours.

Enter Richard, Aumerle, Carlile, and Souldiers.
Rich. Barkloughly Caftle call you this at hand?
Au. Yea, my Lord: how brooks your Grace the ayre,
After your late tofling on the breaking Seas?

4 *Rich.* Needs muft I like it well, I weepe for ioy
To ftand upon my Kingdome once againe.
Deare Earth, I doe falute thee with my hand,
Though Rebels wound thee with their Horfes hoofes:

8 As a long parted Mother with her Child,
Playes fondly with her teares, and fmiles in meeting,
So weeping, fmiling, greet I thee the Earth,
And doe thee favour with my Royall hands,

12 Feed not thy Soueraignes Foe, my gentle Earth,
Nor with thy fweetes comfort his ravenous fence:
           But

of Richard *the second.*

But let thy Spiders that fucke up thy venome,
And heavy-gated Toade lye in their way; † 16
Doing annoyance to the treacherous feete,
Which with ufurping fteps doe trample thee.
Yeild ftinging Nettles to mine Enemies ;
And when they from thy bofome plucke a Flower,
Guard it I prethee with a lurking adder, 20
Whofe double tongue may with a mortall touch
Throw death upon thy Soveraignes Enemies.
Mocke not my fenceleffe Conjuration: Lords ;
This earth fhall have a feeling, and thefe Stones 24
Prove armed Souldiers, ere her native King
Shall falter under fowle Rebellious Armes.

   *Car.*Feare not my Lord,that power that made you King
Hath power to keepe you King, in fpight of all. 28
           33
   *Aum.*He meanes, my Lord,that we are too remiffe,
Whileft *Bullingbrooke* through their fecurity,
Growes ftrong and great, in fubftance and in friends. 36
   Rich. Difcomfortable Cofin, knoweft thou not,
That when the fearching Eye of Heaven is hid
Behinde the Globe,that lights the lower world,
Then theeves and Robbers raunge abroad unfeene, 40
In Murders and in out-rage bloody here :
But when from under this Terreftriall Ball
He fires the proud tops of the Eafterne Pines,
And darts his Lightning through ev'ry guilty hole, 44
Then Murders,Treafons, and detefted finnes
(The Cloake of Night being pluckt from off their backes)
Stand bare and naked, trembling at themfelves.
So when this Thiefe,this Traytor *Bullingbrooke*, 48
Who all this while hath reuell'd in the Night, 50
Shall fee us rifing in our Throne, the Eaft,
His Treafons will fit blufhing in his face, 52
Not able to endure the fight of day;
But felfe-affrighted, tremble at his finne.
Not all the water in the rough rude Sea
Can wafh the Balme from an anoynted King; 56
The breath of worldly men cannot depofe

The Life and Death

The Deputy elected by the Lord :
For every man that *Bullingbrooke* hath preft,
To lift fhrewd Steele againft our Golden Crowne,
60   Heaven for his *Richard* hath in heavenly pay
A glorious Angell : then if Angels fight,
Weake men muft fall, for Heaven ftill guards the right.
    Enter Salisbury.
Welcome my Lord, how farre off lyes your power ?
64   · *Salisb.* Nor neere, nor farther off, my gracious Lord,
Then this weake arme ; difcomfort guides my tongue.
And bids me fpeake of nothing but defpaire :
†   One day to late, I feare (my Noble Lord)
68   Hath clouded all my happy dayes on Earth :
Oh call backe Yefter day, bid time returne,
And thou fhalt have twelve thoufand fighting men :
To day, to day, unhappie day too late
72   Orethrowes thy Ioyes, Friends, Fortune, and thy State.
For all the VVelch-men hearing thou wert dead,
Are gone to *Bullingbrooke*, difperft, and fled.
    Aum. Comfort my Liege, why lookes your Grace fo
pale ?
76   *Rich.* But now the blood of twentie thoufand Men
Did triumph in my face, and they are fled,
And till fo much blood thither come againe,
Have I not reafon to looke pale, and dead ?
80   All foules that will be fafe, flye from my fide,
For time hath fet a blot upon my pride.
    Aum. Comfort my Liege, remember who you are.
    Rich. I had forgot my felfe. Am I not King ?
84   Awake thou fluggard Majefty, thou fleepeft :
Is not the Kings Name forty thoufand Names ?
Arme, arme my Name : a puny fubiect ftrikes
At thy great glory, Looke not to the ground,
88   Ye Favorites of a King : are we not high ?
High be our thoughts : I know my Vncle *Yorke*
Hath Power enough to ferve our turne,
But who comes here ?   *Enter Scroope.*
    Scroope. More health and happineffe betide my Liege,
                  Then

of Richard *the second.*

Then can my care-tun'd tongue deliver him.   *92*

  *Rich.*Mine eare is open,and my heart prepar'd:
The worſt is worldly loſſe, thou canſt unfold :
Say,Is my Kingdome loſt ?why 'twas my Care:
And what loſſe is it to be rid of Care?   *96*
Strives *Bullingbrooke* to be as great as we ?
Greater he ſhall not be : If he ſerve God,
Wee'l ſerve him too ; and be his Fellow ſo.
Revolt our ſubjects ? That we cannot mend,   *100*
They breake their Faith to God as well as us :
Cry Woe,Deſtruction,Ruine,Loſſe,Decay,
The worſt is Death,and death will have his day.

  Scroope Glad am I ,that your Highneſſe is ſo arm'd   *104*
To beare the tidings of Calamity.
Like an unſeaſonable ſtormy day,
Which make the ſilver Rivers drowne their Shores,
As if the world were all diſſolu'd to teares :   *108*
So high, above his Limits, ſwells the Rage
Of *Bullingbrooke*, covering your fearefull Land
With hard bright Steele,and hearts harder then Steele :
White Beares have arm'd their thin and haireleſſe Scalps   *112*
Againſt thy Majeſty, and boyes with womens voyces,
Strive to ſpeake bigge , and clap their female joynts
In ſtiffe unwieldy Armes : againſt thy Crowne
Thy very Beadſ-men learne to bend their bowes   *116*
Of double fatail Eugh : againſt thy ſtate
Yea Diſtaffe-VVomen manage ruſty Bills :
Againſt thy Seat both young and old rebell,
And all goes worſe then I have power to tell.   *120*

  *Rich.*Too well,too well thou tell'ſt a Tale ſo ill.
VVhere is the Earle of Wiltſhire ? where is *Baget* ?
VVhat is become of *Buſhy* ? where is *Greene* ?
That they have let the dangerous Enemy   *124*
Meaſure our Confines with ſuch peacefull ſteps ?
If we prevaile, their hands ſhall pay for it.
I warrant they haue made peace with *Bullingbrooke*.

  Scroope. Peace have they made with him indeede (my   *125*
Lord.)

               F 2   *Rich.*

The Life and Death

Rich, Oh Villaines, Vipers, damn'd without redemption,
Dogs, eafily won to fawne on any man,
Snakes in my heart blood warm'd, that fting my heart,
132   Three Iudaffes, each one thrice worfe then *Iudas*,
Would they make peace? terrible Hell make warre,
Vpon their fpotted foules for this Offence.

    Scroope, Sweet loue (I fee) changing his property,
136   Turnes to the fowreft, and moft deadly hate:
Againe uncurfe their foules : their peace is made
With Heads, and not with hands : thofe whom you curfe
Haue felt the worft of deaths deftroying hand,
140   And lye full low, grav'd in the hollow ground.

    Aum. Is *Bufhy*, *Greene*, and the Earle of Wiltfhire dead
    Scroope. Yea, all of them at Briftow loft their heads.
    Aum. Where is the Duke my Father with his Power:
144   *Rich*. No matter where, of comfort no man fpeake :
Let's talke of Graues, of Wormes, and Epitaphs,
Make duft our Paper, and with Rainy Eyes.
Write forrow in the bofome of the Earth.
148   Let's chufe Executors, and talke of Wills :
And yet not fo ; for what can we bequeath,
Saue our depofed bodies to the ground ?
Our Lands, our liues, and all are *Bullingbrookes*,
152   And nothing can we call our owne, but Death,
And that fmall modell of the barren Earth,
Which ferues as pafte, and couer to our bones:
For Heauens fake let us fit upon the ground,
156   And tell fad ftories of the death of Kings.
How fome haue beene depos'd, fome flaine in warre,
Some haunted by the Ghofts they haue depos'd,
Some poyfon'd by their Wiues, fome fleeping kill'd,
160   All murther'd. For within the hollow Crowne
That rounds the mortall temples of a King,
Keepes Death his Court, and there the Antique fits
Scoffing his ftate, and grinning at his pompe,
164   Allowing him a breath, a little Scene,
To Monarchize, be fear'd, and kill with lookes,
Infuſing him with felfe and vaine conceit,

                                                    As

of Richard *the second.*

As if this Flesh , which walls about our Life,
VVere Braſſe impregnable: and humor'd thus,
Comes at the laſt, and with a little Pinne
Boares through his Caſtle VValls, and farewell King
Cover your heads, and mocke not fleſh and, blood
VVith ſolemne Reverence: throw away Reſpect,
Tradition, forme , and Ceremonious duty,
For you have but miſtooke me all this while:
I live with bread like you , feele VVant,
Taſte Griefe , need Friends : ſubjected thus,
How can you ſay to me, I am a King ?

   *Carl.*My Lord;wiſe men ne're waile their preſent woes,
But preſently prevent the wayes to waile :
To ſeare the Foe,ſince feare oppreſſeth ſtrength,
Gives in your weakeneſſe, ſtrength unto your Foe ;
Feare,and be ſlaine , no worſe can come to ſight ,
And fight and die, is death deſtroying death.
VVhere fearing dying, payes death ſervile breath.

   Aum. My Father hath a Power,enquire of him,
And learne to make a Body of a Limbe.

   Rich. Thou chid'ſt me well:proud *Bullingbrocke* I come
To change blowes with thee, for our day of Doome:
This Ague-fit of feare is over-blowne,
An eaſie taske it is to win our owne.
Say *Scroope*,where lies our Vncle with his Power?
Speake ſweetly man,although thy lookes be ſowre.

   *Scroope.*Men iudge by the complexion of the skie
The ſtate and inclination of the day,
So may you by my dull and heavy Eye:
My tongue hath but a heavier Tale to ſay:
I play the torturer,by ſmall and ſmall
To lengthen out the worſt,that muſt be ſpoken,
Your Vncle *Torke* is joyn'd with *Bullingbrooke*,
And all your Northerne Caſtles yeilded up,
And all your ſoutherne Gentlemen in Armes
Vpon his Faction.

   Rich. Thou haſt ſayd enougn.
Beſhrew thee Coſin, which didſt lead me forth

168

172

176

181
<
183

188

192

196

200

204

The Life and Death

Of that fweet way I was in,to difpaire :
What fay you now? what comfort have we now?
By heaven Ile hate him everlaftingly,
208 That bids me be of comfort any more.
Goe to Flint Caftle,there Ile pine away,
A King,Woes flave,fhall Kingly Woe obey:
That power I have,difcharge,and let 'em goe
212 To eare the Land,that hath fome hope to grow
For I have none. Let no man fpeake againe
To alter this, for counfaile is but vaine.
   Aum. My Liege,one word.
   Rich. He does me double wrong,
216 That wounds me with the flatteries of his tongue,
Difcharge my followers : let them hence away,
From *Richards* Night,to *Bullingbrookes* faire Day. *Exeu.*

Scæna Tertia.

Enter with Drum and Colours,Bullingbrooke,Yorke,
Northumberland, Attendants.
   Bul. So that by this intelligence we learne
The Welchmen are difpers'd, and *Salisbury*
Is gone to meete the King,who lately landed
4 With fome few private friends,upon this Coaft.
   Nor. The news is very faire and good my Lord,
Richard not farre from hence, hath hid his head.
   Yor. It would befeeme the Lord Northumberland,
8 To fay King *Richard*: a lacke the heavy day,
When fuch a facred King fhould hide his head.
   Nor. Your Grace miftakes: onely to be briefe,
† Left I this Title out.
   Yor. The time hath beene,
12 Would you have beene fo briefe with him,he would
Have beene fo briefe with you,to fhorten you,
For taking fo the head ; your whole heads length.
                            Bul.

of Richard *the second.*

Bul. Miſtake not(Vncle) farther than you ſhould.

Yor. Take not (good Coſin) farther than you ſhould,
Leaſt you miſtake, the heavens are ore your head.

Bul. I know it (Vncle) and oppoſe not my ſelfe
Againſt their will. But who comes here ?

Enter Percy.

Welcome *Harry* : what, will not this Caſtle yeeld ?

Per. The Caſtle royally is mann'd, my Lord,
Againſt thy entrance.

Bul. Royally ? Why, it contaynes no King ?

Per. Yes (my good Lord)
It doth containe a King: King *Richard* lyes
Within the limits of yond Lime and Stone,
And with him the Lord *Aumerle*, Lord *Salisbury*
Sir *Stephen Scroope*, beſides a Cleargy man
Of holy reverence : who, I cannot learne.

Nor. Oh, belike it is the Biſhop of Carlile.

Bul. Noble Lord,
Goe to the rude Ribs of that ancient Caſtle,
Through Brazen Trumpet ſend the breath of Parle
Into his ruin'd Eares, and thus deliver :
Henry Bullingbrooke upon his knees doth kiſſe
King *Richards* hand, and ſends allegeance
And true fayth of heart to his royall Perſon: hither come
Even at his feete, to lay my armes and power
Provided, that my Baniſhment repeal'd,
And Lands reſtor'd againe, be freely granted :
If not, ile uſe th'advantage of my power,
And lay the ſummers duſt with ſhowers of blood
Rayn'd from the wounds of ſlaughter'd Engliſhmen;
The which, how farre off from the mind of *Ballingbrooke*
It is, ſuch Crimſon Tempeſt ſhould bedrench
The freſh greene Lap of faire King *Richards* Land
My ſtooping duty tenderly ſhall ſhew.
Goe ſignifie as much, while here we march
Vpon the Graſſie Carpet of this plaine
Let's march without the noyſe of threatning Drum,
That from this Caſtels tatter'd Battelments

Our

16
†
20
24
28
32
36
40
44
48
52

The Life and Death

Our faire Appoyntments may be well perus'd
Me thinkes King Richard and my selfe should meete.
With no lesse terror then the Elements
Of Fire and Water, when their thundering smoake
At meeting teares the cloudy cheekes of Heaven:
Be he the fire, Ile be the yeilding Water;
The rage be his, while on the Earth I raine
My Waters on the Barth, and not on him.
March on, and marke King Richard how he lookes.
 Parle without, and answer within: then a Flourish.
 Enter on the Walls, Richard, Carlile, Aumerle, Scroop,
 Salisbury.

See, see, King Richard doth himselfe appeare
As doth the blushing discontented Sunne,
From out the fiery Portall of the East,
When he perceives the envious clouds are bent
To dimme his glory, and to staine the tract
Of his bright passage to the Occident.

 Tor. Yet lookes he like a King: behold his Eye
(As bright as is the Eagles) lightens forth
Controlling Majesty: alacke, alacke, for woe,
That any harme should staine so faire a show.

 Rich. We are amaz'd, and thus long have we stood
To watch the fearefull bending of thy Knee,
Because we thought our selfe thy lawfull King:
And if we be, how dare thy ioynts forget
To pay the awfull duty of our presence?
If we be not, shew us the hand of God,
That hath dismis'd us from our Stewardship,
For well we know no hand of blood and bone
Can gripe the sacred handle of our Scepter,
Vnlesse he doe prophane, steale or usurpe.
And though you thinke, that all as you have done,
Have torne their soules, by turning them frem us,
And we are barren, and bereft of friends:
Yet know, my master, God Omnipotent,
Is mustring in his Clouds, in our behalfe,
Armies of Pestilence, and they shall strike

         Your

Your Children yet unborne, and unbegot,
That lift your Vaſſall hands againſt my head,
And threat the glory of my precious Crowne.
Tell *Bullingbrooke*, for yond me thinkes he is,
That every ſtride he makes upon my Land,
Is dangerous Treaſon: he is come to ope
The purple Teſtament of bleeding Warre;
But ere the Crowne he lookes for, live in peace,
Ten thouſand bloody crownes of Mothers Sonnes
Shall ill become the flower of Englands face,
Change the complexion of her Maide-pale Peace
To Scarlet indignation, and bedew
Her paſtors Graſſe with faythfull Engliſh blood.
 Nor. The King of Heaven forbid our Lord the King
Should ſo with civill and uncivill Armes
Be ruſht upon: Thy thrice-noble Coſin,
Harry Bullingbrooke, doth humbly kiſſe thy hand,
And by the honourable Tombe he ſweares,
That ſtands upon your Royall Grandſires Bones,
And by the royclties of both your bloods.
(Currents that ſpring from one moſt gracious head)
And by the buried hand of Warlike *Gaunt*,
And by the worth and honour of himſelfe,
Comprizing all that may be ſworne, or ſayd,
His comming hither hath no farther ſcope,
Then for his Lineall Royalties, and to begge
Inſranchiſement-immediate on his knees:
Which on thy Royall party granted once,
His glittering Armes he will commend to ruſt,
His barbed Steeds to ſtables, and his heart
To faythfull ſervice of your Maieſty:
This ſweares he as he is a Prince, is juſt,
And as I am a Gentleman I credit him.
 Rich. Northumberland, ſay thus: The King retures,
His Noble Coſin is right welcome hither,
And all the number of his faire demands
Shall be accompliſh'd without contradiction:
With all the gracious utterance thou haſt,

                  G   Speake

Line numbers in right margin: 88, 92, 96, 100, 104, 108, 112, 116, 120, 124

The Life and Death

Speake to his gentle hearing kind commends.
VVe doe debafe our felfe (Cofin) doe we not,
To looke fo poorely , and to fpeake fo faire ?
Shall we call backe *Northumberland* and fend
Defiance to the Traytor and fo die ?
*Aum.*No,good my Lord,let's fight with gentle words,
Till time lend friends, and friends their hopefull Swords.
Rich. Oh God,oh God,that ere this tongue of mine,
That layd the fentence of dread Banifhment
On yond proud man, fhould take it of againe
VVith words of footh : O that I were as great
As is my Griefe, or leffer than my Name,
Or that I could forget what I have beene,
Or not remember what I muft be now :
Swell'ft thou proud heart ? Ile giue thee fcope to beate,
Since foes have fcope to beate both thee and me.
Au. *Northumberland* comes backe from *Bullingbrooke.*
*Rich.*VVhat muft the King doe now ? muft he fubmit?
The King fhall doe it : Muft he he depos'd ?
The King fhall be contented : Muft he lofe
The Name of King ? o' Gods Name let it goe.
Ile give my Iewels for a fet of beades,
My gorgeous Pallace, for a Hermitage,
My gay Apparrell , for an Almes-mans Gowne,
My figur'd Goblets, for a Difh of Wood,
My Scepter for a Palmers walking Staffe,
My Subjects , for a payre of carved Saints,
And my large Kingdome , for a little Grave,
A little little Grave, an obfcure Grave.
Or Ile be buried in the Kings high-way,
Some way of common Trade, where Subjects feete
May howrely trample on their Soveraignes Head :
For on my heart they tread now , whileft I live ;
And buried once,why not upon my Head ?
Aumerle , thou weep'ft (my tender-hearted Cofin)
VVee'le make foule Weather with defpifed Teares:
Our fighs, and they, fhall lodge the Summer Corne,
And make a Dearth in this revolting Land.

Or

Or ſhall we play the wantons, with our woes,　164
And make ſome pretty match with ſhedding teares?
As thus: to drop them ſtill upon one place,
Till they have fretted us a paire of Graves,
VVithin the Earth: and therein layd, there lies　168
Two Kinſmen digg'd their Graves with weeping Eyes?
VVould not this ill, doe well? well, well, I ſee
I talke but idly, and you mocke at me.
Moſt mighty Prince, my Lord *Northumberland*,　172
VVhat ſayes King *Bullingbrooke*? will his Majeſty
Give *Richard* leave to live, till *Richard* die?
You make a legge and *Bullingbrooke* ſayes I,
　Nor. My Lord, in the baſe Court he doth attend　176
To ſpeake with you, may it pleaſe you to come downe.
　Rich. Downe, downe I come, like gliſt'ring *Phaeton*,
Wanting the manage of unruly Iades.
In the baſe Court? baſe Court where Kings grow baſe,　180
To come at Traytors calls, and doe them grace.　(King,
In the baſe Court come downe: downe Court, downe
For Night-Owles ſhrike, where mounting Larks ſhould
　Bul. What ſayes his Majeſty?　(ſing.
　Nor. Sorrow and griefe of heart　184
Makes him ſpeake fondly, like a franticke man:
Yet he is come.
　Bul. Stand all apart,
And ſhew faire duty to his Maieſty.
My gracious Lord.
　Rich. Faire Coſin,
You debaſe your Princely knee,　190
To make the baſe earth proud with kiſſing it.
Me rather had, my heart might feele your love,
Than my unpleas'd Eye ſee your courteſie.
Vp Coſin, up, your Heart is up, I know,　194
Thus high at leaſt, although your knee below.
　Bul. My gracious Lord, I come but for mine owne.
　Rich. Your owne is yours, and I am yours, and all.
　Bul. So farre be mine, (my moſt redoubted Lord,)　198
As my true ſervice ſhall deſerue your love.
　　　　　G 2　　　　　*Rich.*

The Life and Death

Rich. Well you deſerv'd:
They well deſerue to have,
That know the ſtrong'ſt,and ſureſt way to get,
Vncle give me your hand: nay,dry your eyes,
Teares ſhew their love but want their remidies.
Coſin I am too young to be your Father,
Though you are old enough to be my Heire.
What you will have, I le give, and willing too,
For doe we muſt, what force will have us doe.
Set on towards London:
Coſin,is it ſo?
   Bul. Yea,my good Lord.
   Rich. Then I muſt not ſay no.   *Flouriſh,*   *Exeunt.*

Scæna Quinta.

Enter Queene,and two Ladies.
   Qu. What ſport ſhall we deviſe here in this Garden,
To driue away the heavy thought of Care?
   La. Madam,we'le play at Bowles.
   Qu. 'Twill make me thinke the world is full of Rubs,
And that my fortune runnes againſt the Byas.
   La. Madam, we'le Dance.
   Qu. My legges can keepe no meaſure in Delight,
When my poore heart no meaſure keepes in Griefe.
Therefore no Dancing (Girle) ſome other ſport.
   La. Madam, we'le tell Tales.
   Qu. Of ſorrow, or of griefe?
   La. Of eyther Madam.
   Qu. Of neyther Girle.
For if of ioy,being altogether wanting,
It doth remember me the more of ſorrow:
Or if of griefe,being altogether had,
It addes more ſorrow to my want of joy:
For what I have, I need not to repeat;

                             And

And what I want, it bootes not to complaine.

  La. Madam, Ile fing.

  Qu.'Tis well that thou haſt cauſe ;
But thou ſhould'ſt pleaſe me better,would'ſt thou weepe.
  La. I could weepe,Madam, would it doe you good.
  Qu. And I could fing,would weeping doe me good,
And never borrow any Teare of thee.

Enter a Gardiner, and two Servants.

But ſtay, heere come the Gardiners.
Let's ſtep into the ſhadow of theſe Trees.
My wretchedneſſe,unto a Row of Pinnes,
They'le talke of ſtate : for every one doth ſo,
Againſt a change, Woe is fore-runne with woe.
  *Gard.*Goe binde thou up yond dangling Apricocks.
VVhich like unruly Children,make their Syre
Stoupe with oppreſſion of their prodigall weight ;
Give ſome ſupportance to the bending twigges.
Goe thou, and like an Executioner
Cut off the heads of too faſt growing ſprayes.
That looke too lofty in our Common-wealth:
All muſt be even,in our Governement.
You thus imploy'd, I will goe root away
The noyſome weedes,that without profit ſucke
The Soyles fertility from wholeſome flowers.
  *Ser.*Why ſhould we,in the compaſſe of a Pale,
Keepe Law and Forme, and due Proportion,
Shewing as in a Modell our firme ſtate ?
When our Sea-walled Garden,(the whole Land)
Is full of Weedes,her faireſt Flowers choakt up,
Her Fruit-trees all unpruin'd,her Hedges ruin'd,
Her Knots diſorder'd,and her wholeſome Hearbes
Swarming with Caterpillers.
  Gard. Hold thy peace.
He that hath ſuffer'd this diſorder'd Spring,
Hath now himſelfe met with the Fall of Leafe.
The Weeds that his broad-ſpreading Leaves did ſhelter,
That ſeem'd, in eating him, to hold him up,
Are pull'd up,Root, and all by *Bullingbrooke* ;

G 3   I

I meane the Earle of Wiltſhire, *Buſhy, Greene,*
 Ser. What are they dead ?
 Gard· They are,
And *Bullingbrooke* hath ſeiz'd the waſtefull King.
What pitty is it, that he hath not trim'd
And dreſt his Land, as we this Garden, at time of yeare ;
And wound the Barke, the skin of our Fruite-trees,
Leaſt being over-proud with Sap and Blood,
With too much riches it confound it ſelfe ?
Had he done ſo to great and growing men,
They might have liv'd to beare, and he to taſte
Their fruits of duty. All ſuperfluous branches
We lop away, that bearing boughes may live:
Had he done ſo, himſelfe had borne the Crowne,
Which waſte and idle houres, hath quite throwne downe.
 Ser. VVhat thinke you the King ſhall be depos'd ?
 Gard. Depreſt he is already, and depos'd
'Tis doubted he will be. Letters came laſt night
To a deare friend of the Duke of *Torke,*
That tell blacke tidings.
 Qu. Oh I am preſt to death, through want of ſpeaking:
Thou old *Adams* likeneſſe, ſet to dreſſe this Garden:
How dares thy harſh tongue ſound this unpleaſing
What *Eve,* what ſerpent hath ſuggeſted thee, (newes?
To make a ſecond fall of curſed man ?
Why do'ſt thou ſay King *Richard* is depos'd ?
Dar'ſt thou, (thou little better thing then earth)
Divine his downefall ? Say where, when, and how
Cam'ſt thou by this ill tydings ? Speake thou wretch.
 Gard. Pardon me Madam. Little joy have I
To breath theſe newes ; yet what I ſay, is true ;
King *Richard,* he is in the mighty hold
Of *Bullingbrooke,* their fortunes both are weigh'd :
In your Lords Scale, is nothing but himſelfe,
And ſome few vanities, that make him light :
But in the Ballance of great *Bullingbrooke,*
Beſides himſelfe, are all the Engliſh Peeres,
And with that oddes he weighes King *Richard* downe.
           Poſt

of Richard *the second.*

Poſt you to London, and you'l finde it ſo,
I ſpeake no more,then every one doth know.

   Qu. Nimble miſchance,that art ſo light of foote,   *92*
Doth not thy Embaſſage belong to me?
And am I laſt that know it? Oh thou think'ſt   *1*
To ſerue me laſt, that I may longeſt keepe
Thy ſorrow in my breaſt. Come Ladies goe,   *96*
To meet at London, Londons King in woe.
What,was I borne to this? that my ſad looke
Should grace the Triumph of great *Bullingbrooke!*
Gard'ner, for telling me this newes of woe.   *100*
I would the Plants thou graft'ſt may never grow. *Exit.*

   Gard. Poore Queene, ſo that thy ſtate might be no
I would my skill were ſubiect to thy curſe: (worſe,
Here did ſhe drop a teare, here in this place   *104*
Ile ſet a Banke of Rew,(ſowre Herbe of Grace:)
Rue,ev'n for ruth,here ſhortly ſhall be ſeene,
In the remembrance of a weeping Queene.   *Exit.*

Actus Quartus, Scæna Prima.

Enter as to the Parliament, Bullingbrooke, Aumerle,Nor-
thumberland,Percy,Fitz-Water,Surrey,Carlile,Abbot
of Weſtminſter. Herauld,Officers, and Bagot.

  Bul. Call forth *Bagot.*
Now *Bagot,* freely ſpeake thy mind,
VVhat thou doſt know of Noble *Gloſters* death,
VVho wrought it with the King,and who perform'd   *4*
The bloody Office of his timeleſſe end,
   Bag. Then ſet before my face the Lord *Aumerle.*
   Bul. Coſin,ſtand forth and looke upon that man.
   Bag. My Lord *Aumerle,* I know your daring tongue   *8*
Scornes to unſay what it hath once deliver'd.
In that dead time,when *Gloſters* death was plotted,

                            I

The Life and Death

I heard you fay, Is not my arme of length,
That reacheth from the reſtfull Engliſh Court
As farre as Callis,to my Vncles head ?
Amongſt much other talke,that very time,
I heard you fay,that you had rather refuſe
The offer of an hundred thouſand Crownes.
Then *Bullinghrookes* returne to England; adding withall,
How bleſt this Land would be,in this your Coſins death.

   Aum. Princes and Noble Lords:
What anſwer ſhall I make to this baſe man :
Shall I ſo much diſhonour my faire ſtarres,
On equall termes to give him chaſticement ?
Eyther I muſt,or have mine honour ſpoyl'd
With th' Atteindor of his ſland'rous lips,
There is my Gage,the manuall ſeale of death
That markes thee out for hell. Thou lyeſt,
And will maintaine what thou haſt ſayd,is falſe,
In thy hearts blood,though being all too baſe,
To ſtaine the temper of my Knightly ſword.

   Bul.Bagot forbeare,thou ſhalt not take it up.
   Aum. Excepting one,I would he were the beſt
In all this preſence,that hath moovd me ſo.

   Fitz. If that thy valour ſtand on ſympathies :
There is my Gage, *Aumerle* , in Gage to thine:
By that faire ſunne,that ſhewes me where thou ſtand'ſt,
I heard thee ſay,(and vantingly thou ſpak'ſt it)
That thou wer't cauſe of Noble *Gloſters* death.
If thou denieſt it,twenty times thou lyeſt,
And I will turne thy falſehood to thy heart,
Where it was forged,with my Rapiers poynt.

   Aum. Thou dar'ſt not (Coward) live to ſee the day.
   Fitz. Now by my Soule,I would it were this houre.
   Aum. Fitzwater thou art damn'd to hell for this.
   Per. Aumerle,thou lyeſt: his honour is as true
In this appeale, as thou art all uniuſt:
And that thou art ſo,there I throw my Gage
To proveit on thee,to th' extreameſt poynt
Of mortall breathing. Seize it if thou dar'ſt.

                    Aum.

oj Richard *the second.*

Aum. And if I doe not, may my hands rot off,
And never brandifh more revengefull Steele,
Over the glittering Helme of my Foe.

Sur. My Lord *Fitzwater*:
I doe remember well, the very time
Aumerle, and you did talke.

Fitz. My Lord,
Tis very true : You were in prefence then ;
And you can witneffe with me, this is true.

Sur. As falfe, by heaven,
As heaven it felfe is true. 64

Fitz. Surry, thou lyeft,

Sur. Difhonourable Boy ;
That lye fhall lye fo heavy on my fword,
That it fhall render Vengeance and Revenge,
Till thou the Lye-giver, and that lye, doe lye 68
In earth as quiet, as thy Fathers Scull.
In proofe whereof, there is mine Honours pawne,
Engage it to the Tryall, if thou dar'ft.

Fitz. How fondly doft thou fpurre a forward Horfe? 72
If I dare eate, or drinke, or breath, or live,
I dare meete *Surry* in a Wildernefle,
And fpit upon him, whilft I fay he lies,
And lies, and lies : there is my bond of Faith, 76
To tye thee to my ftrong Correction.
As I intended to thrive in this new world,
Aumerle is guilty of my true appeale.
Befides, I heard the banifh'd *Norfolke* fay, 80
That thou *Aumerle* didft fend two of thy men,
To execute the Noble Duke at Callis.

Aum. Some honeft Chriftian truft me with a Gage,
That *Norfolke* lies, here doe I throw downe this, 84
If he may be repeald, to try his honour.

Bul. Thefe differences fhall all reft under Gage,
Till *Norfolke* be repeal'd : repeal'd he fhall be ;
(And though mine Enemy) reftor'd againe 88
To all his Lands and Seigniories : when hee's return'd,
Againft *Aumerle* we will inforce his Tryall.

H   *Car.*

The Life and Death

Car. That honourable day fhall ne're be feene.
Many a time hath banifh'd *Norfolke* fought
For Iefu Chrift, in glorious Chriftian field
Streaming the Enfigne of the Chriftian Croffe
Againft blacke Pagans, Turkes, and Saracens:
And toyl'd with workes of warre, retyr'd himfelfe
To *Italy* , and there at *Venice* gave
His Body to that pleafant Countries Earth,
And his pure foule unto his Captaine Chrift,
Vnder whofe Colours he had fought fo long.
 Bul. Why Bifhop , is *Norforke* dead ?
 Carl. As fure as I live my Lord.
 Bul. Sweet peace conduct his fweet foule
To the Bofome of good old *Abraham.*
Lords Appealants , your differences fhall all reft under
Till we affigne you to your dayes of Tryall.   (gage,
                                    Enter Torke.
 Torke. Great Duke of Lancafter, I come to thee
From Plume-pluckt *Richard*, who with willing foule
Adopts thee Heire, and his high Scepter yeelds
To the poffeffion of thy Royall Hand.
Afcend his Throne, defcending now from him,
And long live *Henry*, of that Name the Fourth.
 Bul. In Gods Name, Ile afcend the Regall throne,
 Carl. Mary, Heaven forbid.
VVorft in this Royall Prefence may I fpeake,
Yet beft befeeming me to fpeake the truth.
Would God, that any in this Noble Prefence
Were enough Noble to be upright Iudge
Of Noble *Richard*;then true Noblenoffe would
Learne him forbearance from fo foule a Wrong.
What fubject can give fentence on his King ?
And who fits here, that is not *Richards* fubject ?
Theeves are not judg'd, but they are by to heare
Although apparant guilt be feene in them :
And fhall the figure of Gods Majefty,
His Captaine, fteward, Deputy elect,
Anoynted, Crown'd and planted many yeares.

                                                       Be

92

96

100.

104

108

112

116

120

124

Be judg'd by ſubjects,and inferior breath,
And he himſelfe not preſent ? Oh,forbid,it God,
That in a Chriſtian Climate , ſoules refinde
Should ſhew ſo heynous,blacke,obſcene a deed.
I ſpeake to ſubjects, and a ſubject ſpeakes,
Stirr'd up by Heaven,thus boldly for his King.
My Lord of *Hereford* here,whom you call King,
Is a foule Traytor to prowd *Herefords* King.
And if you Crowne him,let me prophecy,
The blood of Engliſh ſhall manure the ground,
And future ages groane for his foule Act.
Peace ſhall goe ſleepe with *Turkes* and Infidels,
And in this Seat of Peace,tumultuous Warres
Shall Kinne with Kinne,and Kinde with Kinde confound,
Diſorder,Horror, Feare,and Mutiny
Shall here inhabite and this Land be call'd
The field of Golgotha, and dead mens ſculls.
Oh, if you reare this Houſe againſt this Houſe
It will the wofulleſt Diviſion prove,
That ever fell upon this curſed Earth.
Prevent it, reſiſt it, let it not be ſo,
Leaſt Child , Childs Children cry againſt you, VVoe.
North. Well have you argu'd Sir : and for your paines.
Of Capitall Treaſon we arreſt you here.
My Lord of Weſtminſter,be it your charge,
To keepe him ſafely,till his day of Tryall.
May it pleaſe you , Lords, to grant the Commons Suit?
Bull. Fetch hither *Richard*,that in common view
He may ſurrender : ſo we ſhall proceede
VVithout ſuſpition.
Yor. I will be his Conduct. *Exit.*
Bull. Lords, you that here are under our Arreſt,
Procure your Sureties for your Dayes of Anſwer:
Little are we beholding to your Love,
And little look'd for at your helping Hands:
Enter Richard and Yorke.
Rich. Alack, why am I ſent for to a King,
Before I have ſhooke off the Regall thoughts

164 Wherewith I reign'd ? I hardly yet have learn'd
To infinuate , flatter , bow , and bend my Knee.
Give Sorrow leave a while , to returne me
To this fubmiffion. Yet I will remember
168 The favors of thefe men : were they not mine ?
Did they not fometime cry, All hayle to me ?
So *Iudas* did to Chrift : but he in twelve,
Found truth in all, but one ; I, in twelve thoufand , none.
172 God fave the King : will no man fay, Amen ?
Am I both Prieft and Clarke ? well then, Amen.
God fave the King , although I be not he:
And yet Amen , if Heaven doe thinke him me.
176 To doe what fervice, am I fent for hither ?
    Yor. To doe that office of thine owne good will,
VVhich tyred Majefty did make thee offer:
The Refignation of thy State and Crowne
180 To *Henry Bullingbrooke.*
    Rich. Give me the Crown. Here Cofin. feize the Crown:
Here Cofin, on this fide my Hand, on that fide thine.
184 Now is this Golden Crowne like a deepe Well,
That owes two Buckets, filling one another,
The emptier ever dancing in the ayre,
The other downe , unfeene , and full of Water :
188 That Bucket downe, and full of Teares am I,
Drinking my Griefes, whilft you mount up on high.
    Bul. I thought you had beene willing to refigne.
    Rich. My Crowne I am , but ftill my Griefes are mine:
192 You may my Glories and my State depofe,
But not my Griefes ; ftill am I King of thofe.
    Bul. Part of your Cares you give me with your Crown.
    Rich. Your Cares fet up, doe not pluck my Cares down.
196 My Care, is loffe of Care, by old Care done,
Your Care , is gaine of Care, by new Care wonne :
The Cares I giue, I have, though given away,
They tend the Crowne, yet ftill with me they ftay :
200   *Bul.* Are you contented to refigne the Crowne ?
    Rich. I no ; no, I : for I muft nothing be :
Therefore no, no, for I refigne to thee.

                          Now,

Now, marke me how I will undoe my felfe.
I give this heauy weight from off my Head,   204
And this unwieldy Scepter from my hand,
The pride of Kingly fway from out my heart.
With mine owne Teares I wafh away my blame,
With mine owne hands I give away my Crowne.   208
With mine owne Tongue deny my facred State,
With mine owne breath releafe all dutious Oathes :
All pompe and Maiefty I doe forfweare:
My Mannors,Rents,Revenews, I forgoe;   212
My Acts,Decrees,and Statutes I deny :
God pardon all Oathes that are broke to me,
God keepe all vowes unbroke are made to thee.
Make me,that nothing haue,with nothing griev'd,   216
And thou withall pleas'd,that haft all atchiev'd,
Long mayft thou live in *Richards* Seate to fit,
And foone lie *Richard* in an earthy pit.
God fave King *Henry*,un-king'd *Richard* fayes,   220
And fend him many yeares of funne-fhine dayes.
What more remaines ?
  Nor. No more: but that you read
Thefe Accufations,and thefe grievous Crymes,
Committed by your perfon,and your followers   224
Againft the ftate,and profit of this Land :
That by confefling them,the foules of men
May deeme,that you are worthily depos'd.
  Rich. Muft I doe fo? and muft I ravell out   228
My weav'd up follyes? Gentle *Northumberland*,
If thy Offences were upon Record,
Would it not fhame thee in fo faire a troupe,
To reade a Lecture of them ? If thou would'ft,   232
There fhould'ft thou find one haynous Article
Containing the depofing of a King,
And cracking the ftrong warrant of an Oath,
Mark'd with a Blot,damn'd in the booke of Heaven.   236
Nay,all of you that ftand and looke upon me,
Whil'ft that my wretchednefle doth bait my felfe,
Though fome of you,with *Pilate* wafh your hands,

                                        Shewing

The Life and Death

240 Shewing an outward pitty : yet you *Pilates*
Have here deliver'd me to my fowre Croffe,
And Water cannot wafh away your finne.
Nor. My Lord difpatch, read o're thefe Articles.
244 *Rich.* Mine eyes are full of teares, I cannot fee :
And yet falt-water blindes them not fo much,
But they can fee a fort of Traytors here.
Nay, if I turne mine eyes upon my felfe,
248 I finde my felfe a Traytor with the reft
For I have given here my foules confent,
T' undecke the pompous body of a King;
Made glory bafe, a foveraigne, a flave ;
252 Proud Maiefty, a fubiect ; State, a Pefant,
Nor. My Lord.
Rich. No Lord of thine, thou haught-infulting man;
No, nor no mans Lord ; I have no Name, no Title ;
256 No, not that Name was given me at the Font,
But 'tis ufurpt : alacke the heavy day,
That I have worne fo many Winters out,
And know not now, what Name to call my felfe.
260 Oh, that I were a mockery, King of Snow,
Standing before the funne of *Bullingbrooke*,
To melt my felfe away in Water-drops :
Good King, great King, and yet not greatly good,
264 And if my word be fterling yet in England,
Let it command a mirror hither ftraight,
That it may fhew me what a face I have,
Since it is Bankrupt of his Maiefty.
268 *Bul.* Goe fome of you, and fetch a Looking Glaffe.
Nor. Read o're this Paper, while the Glaffe doth come.
Rich. Fiend, thou torments me ere I come to Hell.
Bul. Vrge it no more my Lord *Northumberland.*
272 *Nor.* The Commons will not then be fatisfy'd.
Rich. They fhall be fatisfy'd : ile reade enough,
When I doe fee the very Booke indeed,
Where all my finnes are writ, and that's my felfe.
Enter one with a Glaffe.
276 Give me that Glaffe, and therein will I reade.

No

of Richard *the second.*

No deeper wrinkles yet? hath sorrow strucke
So many blowes upon this face of mine,
And made no deeper wounds? Oh flattering Glasse,
Like to my followers in prosperity, 280
Thou doft beguile me. Was this face the face
That every day, under his houfhold Roofe,
Did keepe ten thoufand men? was this the face,
That like the funne did make beholders winke? 284
Is this the face, which fac'd fo many follyes,
That was at laft out-fac'd by *Bullingbrooke* ?
A brittle glory fhineth in this face,
As brittle as the Glory, is the face, 288
For there it is, crackt in an hundred fhivers.
Marke filent King, the Morall of this fport,
How foone my forrow hath deftroy'd my face.
   Bul. The fhadow of your forrow hath deftroy'd 292
The fhadow of your face.
   Rich. Say that againe.
The fhadow of my forrow: ha, lets fee,
'Tis very true, my griefe lyes all within,
And thefe externall manners of laments, 296
Are meerely fhadows to the unfeene griefe,
That fwells with filence in the tortur'd foule:
There lies the fubftance: and I thanke thee King
For thy great bounty, that not onely giv'ft 300
Me caufe to waile, but teacheft me the way
How to lament the caufe. Ile begge one boone,
And then be gone, and trouble you no more.
Shall I obtaine it?
   Bul. Name it, faire Cofin. 304
   Rich. Faire Cofin? I am greater than a King:
For when I was a King, my flatterers
Were then my fubiects; being now a fubiect,
I have a King here to my flatterer: 308
Being fo great, I have no need to begge.
   Bul. Yet aske.
   Rich, And fhall I have?
   Bul. You fhall.

Rich. 310

The Life and Death

Rich. Then give me leave to goe.
Bul. Whither?
Rich. Whither you will, ſo I were from your ſights.
Bul. Goe ſome of you convey him to the Tower.
Rich. Oh good: convey: Conveyers are you all,
That riſe thus nimbly by a true Kings fall.
Bul. On wedneſday next, we ſolemnly ſet downe
Our Coronation; Lords prepare your ſelves.   *Exeunt.*
Abbot. A wofull Pageant haue we here beheld.
Carl. The woe's to come, the children yet un-borne,
Shall feele this day as ſharpe to them as thorne.
Aum. You holy clergy-men, is there no plot
To rid the Realme of this pernicious blot?
Abbot. Before I freely ſpeake my minde herein,
You ſhall not onely take the Sacrament,
To bury mine intents, but alſo to effect
What ever I ſhall happen to deviſe.
I ſee your browes are full of diſcontent,
Your heart of ſorrow, and your eyes of teares,
Come home with me to ſupper, ile lay a plot
Shall ſhew us all a merry day.   *Exeunt.*

Actus Quintus, Scæna Prima.

Enter Queene, and Ladies.
Qu. This way the King will come: this is the way
To *Iulius Cæſars* ill-errected Tower:
To whoſe flint boſome, my condemned Lord
Is doom'd a Priſoner, by proud *Bullingbrooke.*
Here let us reſt, if this rebellious Earth
Have any reſting for her true Kings Queene.
Enter Richard and Gard.
But ſoft, but ſee, or rather doe not ſee,
My faire Roſe wither: yet looke up; behold.
That you in pitty may diſſolue to dew,

And

And wash him fresh againe with true-love teares.
Ah thou the modell where old Troy did stand,
Thou map of honour, thou King *Richards* Tombe,　　*12*
And not King *Richard* : thou most beauteous Inne,
Why should hard-favor'd griefe be lodg'd in thee,
When triumph is become an Ale-house guest ?

　Rich. Ioyne not with griefe, faire Woman, doe not so,　　*16*
To make my end too sudden ; learne good soule,
To thinke our former State a happy dreame,
From which awak'd, the truth of what we are,
Shewes us but this. I am sworne Brother (sweet)　　*20*
To grim necessity ; and he and I
Will keepe a League till Death. High thee to France,
And Cloyster thee in some Religious house :
Our holy lives must win a new worlds Crowne,　　*24*
Which our prophane houres here have stricken downe.

　Qu. What, is my *Richard* both in shape and mind
Transform'd, and weaken'd ? Hath *Bullingbrooke*
Depos'd thine Intellect ? hath he beene in thy heart ?　　*28*
The Lyon dying thrusteth forth his paw,
And wounds the earth, if nothing else, with rage
To be o're-powr'd : and wilt thou, Pupil-like,
Take thy Correction mildly, kisse the Rodde,　　*32*
And fawne on rage with base humility,
Which art a Lyon, and a King of Beasts ?

　Rich. A King of beasts indeed, if aught but beasts,
I had beene still a happy King of Men.　　*36*
Good (sometime Queene) prepare thee hence for France :
Thinke I am dead, and that even heare thou tak'st,
As from my death-bed, my last living leave.
In winters teadious night sit by the fire　　*40*
With good old folkes, and let them tell thee tales
Of woefull ages, long agoe betide :
And ere thou bid goodnight, to quit their griefe,
Tell thou the lamentable fall of me,　　*44*
And send the hearers weeping to their beds :
For why ? the senceleffe Brands will sympathize
The heavy accent of my moving tongue,

I　　　　　　　　　　　　　　　　　　And

And in compaſſion, weepe the ſire out :
And ſome will moūrne in Aſhes, ſome coale-blacke,
For the depoſing of a rightſull King.

Enter Northumberland.

North. My Lord, the mind of *Bullingbrooke* is chang'd.
You muſt to Pomfret, not unto the Tower.
And Madam, there is order ta'ne for you :
VVith all ſwift ſpeed, you muſt away to *France.*

Rich. Northumberland, thou Ladder wherewithall
The mounting *Bullingbrooke* aſcends my Throne,
The time ſhall not be many houres of age,
More than it is, ere foule ſinne, gathering head,
Shall breake into corruption : thou ſhalt thinke,
Though he devide the Realme, and give thee halfe,
It is too little, helping him to all :
He ſhall thinke, that thou which know'ſt the way
To plant unrightfull Kings, wilt know againe.
Being ne're ſo little urg'd, another way,
To plucke him headlong from th' uſurped Throne.
The Love of wicked friends converts to Feare ;
That Feare, to Hate; and Hate turnes one or both,
To worthy Danger, and deſerved Death.

North. My guilt be on my Head, and there an end :
Take leave, and part, for you muſt part forthwith.

Rich. Doubly divorc'd? (bad men) ye violate
A two-fold Marriage ; 'twixt my Crowne, and me,
And then betiwixt me, and my marryed VViſe.
Let me un-kiſſe the Oath 'twixt thee and me ;
And yet not ſo, for with a kiſſe 'twas made
Part us *Northumberland* : I, towards the North,
Where ſhivering Cold and Sickneſſe pines the Clyme :
My Queene to *France* : from whence, ſet forth in pompe,
She came adorned hither like ſweet may ;
Sent backe Hollowmas, or ſhort'ſt of day.

Qu. And muſt we be divided ? muſt we part ?
Rich. I, hand from hand (my Love) and heart frō heart.
Qu. Baniſh us both, and ſend the King with me.
North. That were ſome Love, but little Pollicy.

Qu.

Qu. Then whither he goes thither let me goe·
Rich. So two together weeping, make one Woe,
Weepe thou for me in France ; I, for for thee here:
Better farre off, than nere, be ne're the neere.
Goe, count thy way with fighes, I, mine with Groanes.
    Qu. So longeſt way ſhall have the longeſt moanes.
Rich. Twice for one ſtep ile groane, the way being ſhort,
And piece the way out with a heavy heart.
Come, come, in woing ſorrow let's be briefe,
Since wedding it, there is ſuch length in griefe :
One kiſſe ſhall ſtop our mouthes, and doubly part ;
Thus give I mine, and thus thus take I thy heart.
    Qu. Give me mine owne againe: 'twere no good part,
To take on me to keepe, and kill thy heart.
So, now I have mine owne againe, be gone,
That I may ſtrive to kill it with a groane·
   Rich. We make woe wanton with this fond delay:
Once more adieu; the reſt let ſorrow ſay.   *Exeunt.*

Scæna Secunda.

Enter Yorke, and his Dutcheſſe.
Dut. My Lord, you told me you would tell the reſt,
When weeping made you breake the ſtory off,
Of our two Coſins comming into London.
    Yor. Where did I leave?
    Dut. At that ſad ſtoppe, my Lord·
Where rude miſ-govern'd hands, from windowes tops,
Threw duſt and rubbiſh on King *Richards* head.
    Yor. Then, as I ſayd, the Duke (great *Bullingbrooke*,)
Mounted upon a hot and fiery Steed,
Which his aſpiring Rider ſeem'd to know,
With ſlow, but ſtately pace, kept on his courſe :
While all tongues cri'd, God ſave thee *Bullingbrooke*,
You would have thought the very windowes ſpake,

The Life and Death

So many greedy lookes of young and old,
  Through Casements darted their desiring eyes.
  Vpon his visage ; and that all the walles
16 With painted Imagery had sayd at once,
  Iesu preserve thee, welcome *Bullingbrooke.*
  Whil'st he, from one side to the other turning,
  Bare-headed, lower then his proud Steeds necke,
20 Bespake them thus : I thanke you Countri-men ;
  And thus still doing, thus he past along.
    Dutch. Alas poore *Richard*, where rides he the whilst?
    Yorke. As in a Theater, the eyes of men
24 After a well grac'd Actor leaves the stage,
  Are idlely bent on him that enters next,
  Thinking his prattle to be tedious.
  Even so, or with much more contempt, mens eyes
28 Did scowle on *Richard* ; no man cride, God save him;
  No joyfull tongue gave him his welcome home,
  But dust was throwne upon his sacred head,
  Which with such gentle sorrow he shooke off,
32 His face still combating with teares and smiles
  (The badges of his greefe and patience)
  That had not God (for some strong purpose) steel'd
  The hearts of men, they must perforce have melted,
36 And Barbarisme it selfe have pittied him.
  But Heaven hath a hand in these events,
  To whose high will we bound our calme contents,
  To *Bullingbrooke*, are we sworne Subjects now,
40 Whose State, and Honour, I for aye allow.
      Enter Aumerle.
    Dut. Heere comes my sonne *Aumerle.*
    Yor. Aumerle that was,
  But that is lost, for being *Richards* Friend.
  And Madam, you must call him *Rutland* now;
44 I am in Parliament pledge for his truth,
  And lasting fealty in the new-made King.
    Dut. Welcome my sonne ; who are the Violets now,
  That strew the greene lap of the new-come Spring ?
48 *Aum.* Madam, I know not, nor I greatly care not,
                                  God

God knowes, I had as lieve be none as one·

Yor. Well, beare you well in this new-spring of time,
Leaſt you be cropt before you come to prime· (umphs?
What news from Oxford? Hold thoſe Iuſts and Tri-   52

Aum. For ought I know my Lord they doe.

Yor: You will be there I know.

Aum. If God prevent not, I purpoſe ſo.

Yor. What ſeale is that that hangs without thy boſome   56
Yea, look'ſt thou pale ? Let me ſee the writing·

Aum, My Lord, 'tis nothing.

Yor. No matter then who ſees it,
I will be ſatisfied, let me ſee the writing·

Aum. I do beſeech your Grace to pardon me,   60
It is a matter of ſmall conſequence,
VVhich for ſome reaſons I would not have ſeene.

Yor. VVhich for ſome reaſons ſir, I meane to ſee :
I feare, I feare.

Dut. VVhat ſhould you feare?   64
'Tis nothing but ſome Bond, that he is entred into
For gay apparrell againſt the Triumph.

Yor. Bound to himſelfe ? what doth he with a bond
That he is bound to ? wife, you are a foole.   68
Boy, let me ſee the writing.

Aum. I doe beſeech you pardon me, I may not ſhew it·

Yor. I will be ſatisfied, let me ſee't I ſay: *Snatches it.*   †
Treaſon, foule treaſon, villaine, traytor, ſlave.   72

Dut. VVhat's the matter, my Lord ?

Yor. Hoa, who's within there ; ſaddle my horſe,
Heaven for his mercy what treachery is here ?

Dut. Why, what is't my Lord ?   73

Yor. Give me my boots, I ſay ; Saddle my horſe :
Now by my honour, my life, my troth·
I will appeach the villaine·

Dut. What is the matter ?

Yor. Peace fooliſh woman.   80

Dut. I will not peace, what is the matter ſonne ?

Aum. Good mother be content, it is no more
Then my poore life muſt anſwer·

The Life and Death

Dut. Thy life anſwer?

Enter Servant with Boots.

84 *Yor.* Bring my Boots, I will unto the King.

Dut. Strike him *Aumerle.* Poore boy,thou art amaz'd,
Hence Villaine,never more come in my ſight.

Yor. Give me my Boots I ſay.

88 *Dut.* Why *Yorke*,what wilt thou doe?
Wilt thou not hide the treſpaſſe of thine owne?
Have we more ſonnes? Or are we like to have?
Is not my teeming date drunke up with time?

92 And wilt thou plucke my faire ſonne from mine Age,
And rob me of a happy mothers name?
Is he not like thee? is he not thine owne?

† *Yor.* Thou fond and mad woman,

96 Wilt thou conceale this darke conſpiracy?
A dozen of them here have tane the Sacrament,
And enterchangeably ſet downe their hands
To kill the King at Oxford.

Dut. He ſhall be none:

100 Wee'l keepe him here: then what is that to him:

Yor. Away fond woman: were he twenty times my
ſonne,I would appeach him.

Dut. Hadſt thou groan'd for him, as I have done,
Thou wouldeſt be more pittifull:

104 But now I know thy minde; thou do'ſt ſuſpect
That I have beene diſloyall to thy bed,
And that he is a baſtard, not thy ſonne:
Sweet *Yorke*, ſweet husband, be not of that mind:

106 He is as like thee, as a man may be,
Not like to me, nor any of my Kin,
And yet I love him.

Yor. Make way,unruly woman. *Exit.*

Dut. After *Aumerle.* Mount thee upon his Horſe,

112 Spurre poſt,and get before him to the King,
And beg thy pardon,ere he doe accuſe thee,
Ile not be long behinde: though I be old,
I doubt not but to ride as faſt as Yorke:

116 And never will I riſe up from the ground,

Till

of Richard *the* *fecond*.

Till *Bullingbroke* have pardon'd thee: Away, be gone, *Ex*.

Sc*æ*na *Tertia*.

Enter Bullingbrooke, Percy, and other Lords.

Bul. Can no man tell of my unthrifty fonne ?
'Tis full three monthes fince I did fee him laft.
If any plague hang over us, 'tis he:
I would to heaven (my Lords) he might be found,
Enquire at London, 'mongft the Tavernes there :
For there (they fay) he daily doth frequent,
With un-reftrained loofe Companions,
Even fuch (they fay) as ftand in narrow Lanes,
And rob our watch, and beate our paffengers,
Which he (young wanton, and effeminate Boy)
Takes on the poynt of honour , to fupport
So diffolute a crew.

Per. My Lord, fome two dayes fince I faw the Prince,
And told him of thefe triumphes held at Oxford.

Bul. And what fayd the Gallant ?

Per. His anfwer was, he would unto the ftewes,
And from the common'ft creature plucke a glove
And weare it as a favour , and with that
He would unhorfe the luftieft challenger.

Bul. As diffolute as defp'rate, yet through both,
I fee fome fparks of better hope: which elder dayes
May happily bring forth. But who comes here ?

Enter Aumerle.

Aum. Where is the King ?

Bul. What meanes my Cofin, that he ftares
And lookes fo wildely ?   (iefty

Aum. God fave your Grace, I doe befeech your Ma-
To have fome conference with your Grace alone.

Bul. Withdraw your felves, and leave us here alone,
What is the the matter with our Cofin now ?

Aum.

The Life and Death

Aum. For ever may my knees grow to the earth,
My tongue cleave to my roofe within my mouth,
Vnlesse a pardon, ere I rise or speake.

Bul. Intended or committed was this fault?
If on the first, how hainous ere it be,
To winne thy after-love I pardon thee.

Aum. Then give me leave, that I may turne the key,
That no man enter till the tale be done.

Bul. Have thy desire.   *Yorke within.*

Yor. My Liege beware, looke to thy selfe,
Thou hast a Traytor in thy presence there.

Bul. Villaine, ile make thee safe.   *feare.*

Aum. Stay thy revengefull hand, thou hast no cause to

Yor. Open the doore, secure foole-hardy King:
Shall I for love speake treason to thy face?
Open the doore, or I will breake it open.   *Enter Yorke.*

Bul. What is the matter (Vncle) speake, recover breath,
Tell us how neere is danger,
That we may arme us to encounter it.

Yor. Peruse this writing here, and thou shalt know
The reason that my haste forbids me show.

Aum. Remember as thou read'st, thy promise past:
I doe repent me reade not my name there,
My heart is not confederate with my hand.

Yor. It was (villaine) ere thy hand did set it downe.
I tore it from the traytors bosome, King.
Feare and not loue, begets his penitence;
Forget to pitty him, least thy pitty prove
A serpent that will sting thee to the heart.

Bul. Oh heinous, strong, and bold conspiracy,
O loyall Father of a trecherous Sonne:
Thou sheere, immaculate, and silver fountaine,
From whence this streame, through muddy passages
Hath had his current, and defil'd himselfe.
Thy overflow of good, converts to bad,
And thine abundant goodnesse shall excuse
This deadly plot, in thy digressing sonne.

Yor. So shall my vertue be his vices bawd,

And

And he shall spend mine Honour, with his shame : 68
As thriftlesse Sonnes their scraping Fathers Gold.
Mine honour lives when his dishonour dyes,
Or my sham'd life in his dishonour lies :
Thou kill'st me in his life, giving him breath, 72
The Traitor lives, the true man's put to death
Dutchesse within.
*Dut.*What hoa (my Liege) for Heavens sake let me in.
*Bul.*What shrill-voic'd suppliant makes this eager cry ?
*Dut.*A Woman and thine Aunt (great King) 'tis I. 76
Speake with me ; pitty me, open the doore,
A begger begs, that never begg'd before.
Bul. Our Scene is alter'd from a serious thing,
And now chang'd to the begger, and the King : 80
My dangerous Cosin, let your Mother in,
I know she's come to pray for your foule sin.
Yor. If thou do pardon, whosoever pray,
More sinnes for this forgivenesse, prosper may. 84
This fester'd joynt cut off, the rest rests sound,
This let alone, will all the rest confound. *Enter Dutchesse.*
Dut. O King, beleeve not this hard-hearted man,
Love, loving not it selfe, none other can. 88
Yor. Thou franticke woman, what dost thou make here,
Shall thy old dugges once more a Traitor reare ?
Dut. Sweet *Yorke* be patient, heare me gentle Liege.
Bul. Rise up good Aunt.
Du. Not yet, I thee beseech. 92
For ever will I kneele upon my knees,
And never see day that the happy sees,
Till thou give joy : untill thou bid me ioy,
By pardoning *Rutland*, my transgressing Boy. 96
Aum. Vnto my Mothers prayers, I bend my knee.
Yorke. Against them both, my true joynts bended be. 98
Dut. Pleades he in earnest ? Looke upon his Face, 100
His eyes do drop no teares : his prayers are in jest :
His words come from his mouth, ours from our breast
He prayes but faintly, and would be deny'd,
VVe pray with heart, and soule, and all beside : 104

K His

The Life and Death

His weary joynts would gladly rife, I know,
Our knees fhall kneele, till to the ground they grow:
His prayers are full of falfe hypocrify,
Ours of true zeale, and deepe integrity:
Our prayers do out-pray his, then let him have
That mercy which true prayers ovght to have.
  Bul. Good Annt ftand up.
  Dut. Nay, doe not fay ftand up.
But pardon firft, and afterwards ftand up.
And if I were thy Nurfe thy tongue to teach,
Pardon fhould be the firft word of thy fpeech.
I never long'd to heare a word till now:
Say Pardon (King,) let pitty teach thee how.
The word is fhort, but not fo fhort as fweet,
No word like Pardon, for Kings mouth's fo meet.
  Yor. Speake it in French, (King) fay, *Pardon'ne moy.*
  Dut. Doft thou teach pardon, Pardon to deftroy?
Ah my fowre husband, my hard-hearted Lord,
That fet'ft the word it felfe, againft the word.
Speake pardon as 'tis currant in our Land,
The chopping French we doe not underftand.
Thine eye begins to fpeake, fet thy tongue there;
Or in thy pittious heart, plant thou thine eare.
That hearing how your plaints and prayers doe pearce,
Pitty may move thee, pardon to rehearfe.
  Bul. Good Aunt ftand up.
  Dut. I doe not fue to ftand,
Pardon is all the fuit I have in hand.
  Bul. I pardon him as heaven fhall pardon me,
  Dut. O happy vantage of a kneeling knee:
Yet am I ficke for feare, fpeake it againe,
Twice faying pardon, doth not pardon twaine,
But makes one pardon ftrong.
  Bul. I pardon him with all my heart.
  Dut. A God on earth thou art.
  Bul. But for our trufty brother-in-law, the Abbot,
With all the reft of that conforted crew,
Deftruction ftraight fhall dogge them at the heeles.
                                        Good

of Richard *the second.*

Good Vncle helpe to order feverall powers
To Oxford, or where ere thefe traytors are :
They fhall not live within this world I fweare,   142
But I will have them if I once knew where.
Vncle farewell , and Cofin too adieu :
Your mother well hath pray'd, and prove you true.
*Dut.*Come my old fon,I pray heaven make thee new.   146
        Enter Exton, and Servant.   *Exit.*
*Ex.*Didft thou not marke the King what words he fpake.
Have I no friend will rid me of this living feare :
Was it not fo ?
   Ser. Thofe were his words.
   Ex. Have I no friend (quoth he) he fpake it twice,   4
And urg'd it twice together did he not ?
   *Ser.*He did.
   Ex. And fpeaking it he wiftly look'd on me,
As who fhould fay,I would thou wer't the man,   8
That would divorce this terror from my heart,
Meaning the King at Pomfret : Come,let's goe,
I am the Kings friend, and will rid his Foe.   *Exit.*   11

Scæna Quarta.

        Enter Richard.
   Rich. I have beene ftudying how to compare
This Prifon where I liue,unto the world :
And for becaufe the world is populous,
And here is not a creature, but my felfe,   4
I cannot doe it : yet ile hammer't out.
My braine, ile prove the female to my Soule
My foule,the Father : and thefe two beget
A generation of ftill breeding thoughts ;   8
And thefe fame thoughts, people this little world
In humors like the people of this world,
For no thought is contented. The better fort,
                K 2   As

As thoughts of things Divine, are intermixt
With scruples, and do set the Faith it selfe
Against the Faith ; as thus Come little ones ; and then
It is as hard to come, as for a Camell   (againe,
To thred the posterne of a Needles eye.
Thoughts tending to Ambition, they do plot
Vnlikely wonders ; how these vaine weake nailes
May teare a passage through the Flinty ribbes
Of this hard world, my ragged prison walles ;
And for they cannot, dye in their owne pride.
Thoughts tending to Content, flatter themselves,
That they are not the first of Fortunes slaves,
Nor shall not be the last. Like silly Beggars,
Who sitting in the Stockes , refuse that shame
That many have, and others must sit there ;
And in this thought, they finde a kind of ease,
Bearing their owne misfortune on the backe
Of such as have before indur'd the like.
Thus play I in one Prison, many people,
And none contented. Sometimes am I King ;
Then Treason makes me wish my selfe a Begger,
And so I am. Then crushing penury,
Perswades me, I was better when a King ;
Then am I king'd againe ; and by and by,
Thinke that I am un-king'd by *Bullingbrooke,*
And straight am nothing. But what ere I am,   *Musicke.*
Nor I, nor any man, that but man is,
With nothing shall be pleas'd, till he be eas'd
With being nothing. Musicke doe I heare ?
Ha,ha ? keepe time ; How sowre sweet Musicke is,
When time is broke, and no Proportion kept ?
So is it in the Musicke of mens lives :
And here have I the daintinesse of eare,
To heare time broke in a disorder'd string :
But for the Concord of my State and time,
Had not an eare to heare my true Time broke.
I wasted Time, and now doth Time waste me :
For now hath time made me his numbring Clocke :

My

of Richard *the second.*

My thoughts,are minutes ; and with fighes they iarre,
There watches to mine eyes the outward Watch,
Whereto my finger,like a Dialls point,
Is poynting ftill, in clenfing them from teares.
Now fir,the found that tels what houre it is,
Are clamorous grones, that ftrike upon my heart,
Which is the bell : fo fighes and teares, and grones,
Shew minutes, houres, and times : O but my time
Runs poafting on,in *Bullingbrookes* proud ioy,
While I ftand fooling here, his jacke o'th' Clocke.
This Muficke mads me, let it found no more,
For though it have holpe mad men to their wits,
In me it feemes,it will make wife-men mad :
Yet bleffing on his heart that gives it me ;
For 'tis a figne of love, and love to *Richard,*
Is a ftrange brooch,in this all-hating world.

Enter Groome.

Groo. Haile Royall Prince.
Rich. Thankes Noble Peere.
The cheapeft of us,is ten grotes to deare.
What art thou ? And how com'ft thou hither ?
Where no man ever comes,but that fad dogge
That brings me food,to make misfortune live ?
Groo. I was a poore Groome of thy ftable (King)
When thou wer't King,who travelling towards Yorke,
VVith much adoo, at length have gotten leave
To looke upon my (fometimes Royall) mafters face.
O how it yern'd my heart,when I beheld
In London ftreets, that Corronation day,
VVhen *Bullingbrooke* rode on Roane Barbary,
That Horfe, that thou fo often haft beftrid,
That Horfe, that I fo carefully haue dreft.
Rich, Rode he on Barbary ? tell me gentle friend,
How went he under him ?
Groo. So proudly,as if he had difdain'd the ground.
Rich. So proud,that *Bullingbrooke* was on his backe ;
That jade hath eate bread from my Royall hand.
This hand hath made him proud with clapping him.

K 3·   VVould

52

66

60

64

68

72

76

80

84

Would he not ftumble ? would he not fall downe
(Since pride muft have a fall) and breake the necke
Of that proud man,that did ufurpe his backe?
Forgiveneffe horfe ; why do I raile on thee,
Since thou created to be aw'd by man
Was't borne to beare?I was not made a horfe
And yet I beare a burthen like an Affe,
Spur-gall'd,and tyr'd by jauncing *Bullingbrooke,*

    Enter Keeper with a difh.

 Keep. Fellow,give place, here is no longer ftay.
 Rich. If thou love me, 'tis time thou wer't away.
 Groo, What my tongue dares not , that my heart fhall
fay.   *Exit.*
 Keep. My Lord wilt pleafe you to fall too?
 Rich. Tafte of it firft, as thou wer't wont to doo.
 Keep. My Lord I dare not: Sir *Percy* of Exton,
Who lately came from th King, commands the contrary.
 Rich. The divell take *Henry* of Lancafter, and thee;
Patience is ftale and I am weary of it.
 Keep. Helpe, helpe, helpe.

    Enter Exton and Servants.

 Ri. How now? what meanes death in this rude affault?
Villaine, thine owne hand yeilds thy deaths inftrument,
Goe thou and fill another roome in hell.

       Exton ftrikes him downe.

That hand fhall burne in never-quenching fire,
That ftaggers thus my perfon. *Exton,* thy fierce hand,
Hath with the Kings blood,ftain'd the Kings owne land.
Mount,mount my foule,thy feate is up on high,
Whil'ft my groffe flefh finkes downeward here to dye.
 Ex. As full of valour as of Royall blood.
Both have I fpilt: Oh would the deed were good,
For now the divell,that told me I did well,
Sayes that this deed is Chronicled in hell.
This dead King to the living King ile beare,
Take hence the reft, and give them buriall here.   *Exit.*

            Scena

Scæna Quinta.

Flourish, *Enter Bullingbrooke,* *Yorke,* *with*
other Lords, and Attendants.

Bul. Vncle Yorke, the latest newes we heare,
Is that the Rebels have confum'd with fire
Our Towne of Ciceter in Glocestershire,
But whether they be tane or flaine, we heare not 4

Enter Northumberland.

VVelcome my Lord, what is the newes?
Nor. Firft, to thy facred ftate, wifh I all happineffe:
The next newes is, I have to London fent
The heads of *Salisbury,* *Spencer,* *Blunt,* and *Kent:* 8
The manner of their taking may appeare
At large difcourfed in this paper here.
Bul. We thanke thee gentle *Percy* for thy paines,
And to thy worth will adde right worthy gaines. 12

Enter Fitz-water. †

Fitz. My Lord, I have from Oxford fent to London,
The heads of *Broccas,* and Sir *Bennet Seely,*
Two of the dangerous conforted Traitors,
That fought at Oxford, thy dire overthrow. 16
Bul. Thy paines *Fitz-water,* fhall not be forgot, †
Right Noble is thy merit, well I wot.

Enter Percy, *and Carlile.*

Per. The grand confpirator, *Abbot* of *Westminster,*
VVith clog of confcience, and fowre melancholly, 20
Hath yeilded up his body to the graue,
But here is *Carlile,* living to abide
Thy Kingly doome, and fentence of his pride.
Bul. *Carlile,* this is your doome: 24
Choofe out fome fecret place, fome reverend roome
More than thou haft, and with it joy thy felfe:
So as thou liv'ft in peace, dye free from ftrife:

For

The Life and Death

28
For though mine enemy thou haſt ever beene,
High ſparkes of honour in thee I have ſeene.
Enter Exton with a Coffin.
Exton. Great King, within this Coffin I preſent
Thy buried feare. Herein all breathleſſe lies
32
The mightieſt of thy greateſt enemies
Richard of Burdeaux, by me hither brought.
Bul. Exton, I thanke thee not, for thou haſt wrought
A deed of ſlaughter, with thy fatall hand.
36
Vpon my head, and all this famous Land.
Ex. From your owne mouth my Lord, did I this deed.
Bul. They love not poyſon, that doe poyſon need,
Nor doe I thee : though I did wiſh him dead,
40
I hate the murtherer, love him murthered.
The guilt of conſcience take thou for thy labour,
But neyther my good word, nor Princely favour.
VVith *Caine* goe wander through the ſhade of night,
44
And never ſhew thy head by day, nor light.
Lords, I proteſt my ſoule is full of woe,
That blood ſhould ſprinkle me, and make me grow,
Come mourne with me, for that I doe lament,
48
And put on ſullen blacke incontinent:
Ile make a voyage to the Holy-land.
To waſh this blood off from my guilty hand
March ſadly after, grace my mourning here,
52
In weeping after this untimely beere. *Exeunt.*

FINIS.

www.ingramcontent.com/pod-product-compliance
Lightning Source LLC
Chambersburg PA
CBHW032358020726
47499CB00008B/2808